WITHOUT REFUGE

WITHOUT REFUGE

JANE MITCHELL

CAROLRHODA BOOKS
MINNEAPOLIS

First American edition published in 2018 by Carolrhoda Books

Text copyright © 2017 by Jane Mitchell

First published in Dublin, Ireland in 2017 by Little Island as *A Dangerous Crossing*

Carolrhoda Books
A division of Lerner Publishing Group, Inc.
241 First Avenue North
Minneapolis, MN 55401 USA

For reading levels and more information, look up this title at www.lernerbooks.com.

Cover and interior images: Secondcorner/Shutterstock.com (background); Chalermsak/Shutterstock.com (silhouette of boy); Emre Tarimcioglu/Shutterstock.com (letters).

Main body text set in Bembo Std regular 12.5/17.
Typeface provided by Monotype Typography.

Library of Congress Cataloging-in-Publication Data

Names: Mitchell, Jane (Writer of books for young people), author.
Title: Without refuge / by Jane Mitchell.
Other titles: Dangerous crossing
Description: Minneapolis : Carolrhoda Books, [2018] | Originally published: Dublin : Little Island Books, 2017 under the title Dangerous crossing. | Summary: Forced to leave his home in war-torn Syria, thirteen-year-old Ghalib makes an arduous journey with his family to a refugee camp in Turkey. Includes glossary.
Identifiers: LCCN 2017026040| ISBN 9781541500501 (lb) | ISBN 9781541510548 (ebk pdf)
Subjects: | CYAC: Refugees—Fiction. | Kurds—Fiction. | Muslims—Fiction. | Family life—Syria—Fiction. | IS (Organization)—Fiction. | Syrians—Turkey—Fiction. | Syria—History—Civil War, 2011—Fiction.
Classification: LCC PZ7.M69265 Dan 2018 | DDC [Fic]—dc23

LC record available at https://lccn.loc.gov/2017026040

Manufactured in the United States of America
1-43679-33486-11/6/2017

DEDICATED TO EVERY SYRIAN CHILD
WHOSE LIFE HAS BEEN DAMAGED,
CHANGED OR BLIGHTED BY THE
SYRIAN CIVIL WAR

1

I sprint around the perimeter of Freedom Square in the center of Kobani. I hardly recognize this place any more, it's such a wreck now. I hug my bundle close: women's shoes and men's shirts, mobile phones in boxes, coloring books only a little bit scorched. Even bicycle parts—all left in the blown-out shops and bombed stalls of the old *souq*. I glance over my shoulder to check that no shopkeepers are chasing me. You'd be surprised how fast they move, considering the size of them, but they've never managed to catch us. We're way too fast for them. I squeeze into the shadow of rubble heaps and ruined buildings. Leap past yawning bomb craters and snarls of rusted steel, over spent bullets and shell casings. I am Ghalib. I am invincible.

My cousin Hamza runs ahead of me. He ducks away from the square and into the narrow streets.

Before I follow, I stop at the gable end of a bombed-out block to wait for my little brother.

"Come on, Alan," I say.

He stops running when he sees me waiting, his red sweater vivid against the dusty streets. He wipes his nose on his sleeve.

"I'm tired, Ghalib," he says.

His left leg kicks a spit of dust with every step. His lopsided walk is worse when he's tired. His bad hand curls into a small hook-shape.

"Straighten your hand," I say.

Hamza comes back to where I wait. My muscles tense. I wish he would go on ahead.

Hamza looks at Alan. "You shouldn't have brought him," he says.

"Shut up, Hamza."

"He'll get us caught."

"He's doing fine."

"He's too slow."

"You don't have to wait for us."

But Hamza waits. He shades his eyes with his hand. He scans the empty streets, the empty sky. He does it to try and pressure me. Shopkeepers come fast if they see us snatching damaged goods, but airstrikes come faster, screaming out of the sky to pulverize everything. When Alan reaches us, I take a box of shoes and two mobile phone boxes from him to stack on top of my stuff. He's left with a box of shoes and a plastic bag of bicycle bells.

"You carry those," I say.

We walk slowly now, sandals crunching on broken stones and rubble. We pick our way around crumpled cars and shattered glass. When the road is blocked with fallen masonry from a collapsed building, Hamza scrambles over the scorched bricks. I hand him our goods, then pull Alan past gaping holes and lumps of concrete.

"Stay away from exposed cables," I say.

Fat flies rise from stinking holes where dead bodies rot beneath smoking ruins. As I lift Alan to the ground, a mild vibration shudders the twists of rusting steel poking from the massive slabs. The metal sings and moans like grieving women. My heart beats harder. I grip Alan's hand. All three of us stop. We wait. We listen. It might be nothing.

We hold our breath in the silence. Shards of broken glass in a window frame chime, trembling and shivering like distant bells. It's not good. The darkness crouching inside me seeps through my blood.

We clutch our bundles closer. I look up at the empty sky. Alan looks at me, eyes wide.

"I want Dayah." He always calls for our mother when he's frightened.

"I want shelter!" Hamza says.

I pull Alan's hand. "Come on."

The faint vibration has already been drowned by the faraway whine. It climbs higher. My chest tightens. We run now, hunting for shelter, panic adding speed to Alan's crooked run. The hammering of our feet is the only sound other than the rising scream of the approaching airstrike. It splinters the waiting air. Cracks open the quiet of the empty streets.

I hurl myself through a gaping hole punched in the wall of what used to be the central library. Hamza and Alan follow. I shove Alan against the scorched wall beneath an overhang of bricks and crumbling mortar. Hamza crawls in next to us. We crouch tight and hard in the corner, breath panting, hearts hammering. Alan trembles beneath me. Maybe Hamza was right. Maybe I should have left Alan at home, especially with an airstrike coming. Dayah will kill me if he gets blown up.

The air swells and shudders. A flash of darkness blinks across the sun as the weapon screams over our heads to smash into the ground far beyond where we huddle. A shuddering rumble passes through us, beneath us. The deep earth itself convulses. The remaining library walls tremble and shake, scattering dust and loose stones over us. Then comes a brief silence—the familiar stillness after a strike. It rushes in, hot and insistent. It crams my throbbing ears. I lift my head. Wait for the chaos to unfold. Hamza sits up too, head white with dust. Alan coughs and spits grit. I grab him and pull him upright to check him over. He doesn't cry or even speak. He stares blankly, eyelashes thick with fine powder. I brush dirt and dust from his dark hair. Wipe his grimy face.

"I want Dayah," Alan says.

"We'll go now," I say, relieved he can still speak.

We need to get moving before the bedlam that always follows an airstrike tears the place apart. I take his hand. We clamber from our makeshift shelter, brushing down our jeans and sweaters. We stare at the towering column of black smoke twisting upward from the city's newest bomb site. None of us speaks. The excitement of looting has run out of us, knocked aside by the airstrike and a sudden hunger to get home. We snatch up some of our scattered goods—they don't seem so important anymore—and make our way past blown-out shops and businesses. Buildings spill broken walls and splintered roofs across our path. People appear in ones and twos from structures shattered in other strikes. They emerge from curtained doorways. Watch us through broken windows.

"Get home to your families," a man says. "You shouldn't be out on the streets."

Others perch high on crumbling balconies to peer across the city. The reek of burning fuel reaches us now, pushing aside the normal stink that fills the broken streets, of rotting food and smashed sewers and bodies.

"Came down near the stadium," a woman says from half a room two stories up.

"Near the business center," another says.

We don't talk and we don't stay to listen. Our bodies tremble. Our ears ring. We hurry back to the Kurdish district where we live. I shift the goods in my arms to take Alan's hand.

"Nearly there," I say. I keep him moving.

I see Dayah and my sister Bushra before they see us. They run up the narrow street, peering down side alleys, stopping to check doorways, gazing again and again at that tower of black smoke. Dayah's face wears the frantic look she always has now. A twist of guilt tightens my belly. Bushra just looks annoyed. That's Bushra's permanent expression. I'll be in trouble for leaving the neighborhood. I'll be in more trouble for going with Hamza. I'll be in most trouble of all for bringing Alan with me. *Maybe Dayah would like a pair of new shoes*, I think. I peer at the boxes in my arms, searching for women's shoes.

When they see us, they stop running. Dayah stands in the middle of the street, headscarf held to her mouth, eyes locked on us. Bushra scowls at me.

"Hi, Aunt Gardina," Hamza says. "Hi, Bushra." He grins like there's nothing wrong. Bushra glares at Hamza; Dayah ignores him. Her gaze is fixed on me.

"Where did you take him?" she says.

I hear anger and relief, sadness and terror, woven all at once through her words.

"Dayah!" Alan says. He releases my hand and runs into her outstretched arms.

"See you later, Ghalib," Hamza says to me. He heads for his own home.

Dayah drops to her haunches and snatches Alan to her. She examines him fiercely, running her hands over his dusty body, feeling the shape of his skull with her fingertips, turning him around to lift his sweater and check his spine, his smooth undamaged skin. He is her precious baby who nearly didn't live to be her precious boy. She caresses his two arms, pausing over the weaker left one, and his skinny legs, touching his scuffed knees, lingering over his gimpy leg. Only when she's certain he is uninjured and just filthy and frightened, does she hug him tightly to her. She grips him like she'll never let him go. She breathes in the fear that rises from him with the grit and dust. She presses her face to the top of his head, her headscarf coated in the grime from his dust-thick hair, the front of her dress imprinted with his sooty silhouette.

All the while she examines him, I watch them. I say nothing. Alan submits to the inspection without resistance or questioning. There's comfort for both of them in the grooming, the checking over, the safe return. I'm not part of it. I'm too old for my mother to run her hands over my body, but as I watch them, something vivid and sweet blossoms in my memory. I know she doesn't have the same love for me right now after I sneaked Alan away from her and brought him into the city, where airstrikes and barrel bombs scorch through the sky.

I don't look at Bushra. I know what her expression will be like and I don't want to see it. She ignores me. My sister has little time for me.

Dayah turns to me at last. It was only a matter of time. "And you," she says.

I brace myself. I meet her eye. I stand straight.

"How dare you take him into the city!" Fury flashes from her words like the glint of a new knife.

"I brought you shoes, Dayah," I say. I hold out a box of shoes. She ignores it.

"Look!" she says. She sweeps her hand toward the towering column of black smoke, snatched now by air currents so it smears its oily filth across the sky above the city. Fire alarms and the dull thump of explosions at ground level fill the silence between her words.

"Look!" she says again. She gestures toward Alan, grimy with concrete dust and smudged with dirt.

"It didn't hit the souq," I say.

"I don't care where it hit, Ghalib. Look at the state of your brother. You could have been blown to pieces."

"But we weren't. And we got good stuff." I try again. "Look at the nice shoes I got you."

"Seriously, Ghalib?" Bushra says. She turns away from me in disgust.

"I don't want shoes, Ghalib!" Dayah says. "I don't want you going downtown with Hamza to loot and steal. It's wrong! We didn't raise you to be a thief. And it's worse that you're teaching your brother."

We start walking toward home. Alan holds Dayah's hand. "I suppose this was Hamza's idea," she says.

"It wasn't Hamza's idea," I say.

"Do you always have to copy whatever he does?" Dayah says. "It's usually something bad. Why can't you keep your head about you, Ghalib?"

"I made him do it, Dayah," Alan says in a small voice. Dayah looks at Alan. Bushra looks at Alan. I look at Alan. "I told Ghalib I would tell you he was going to the souq with Hamza if he didn't take me along."

He's a good liar. Even I'm convinced. Dayah's eyes soften as she looks at him. Everyone softens when they look at Alan. Something about him makes people want to care for him. Dayah bends down and picks him up. He's definitely too old to be carried but he gets away with it.

"You're never to go to the souq with Ghalib again," Dayah says to him.

And as we walk home, I think Alan might be useful to bring along next time. He might keep me out of trouble.

2

Our *mukhtar* is a smart man. As soon as we heard whispers of ISIS coming to Kobani, he gathered up a group of men from our neighborhood and traveled to the industrial center on the outskirts of the city. They bought a dozen electricity generators and drums of diesel with the utility allowance from the city council, brought them home in a convoy of minibuses, and locked them into the storage sheds behind the mosque. Plenty of people were furious about it.

"What a waste of money," some said. "ISIS will be gone in six months and we'll have no money to repair potholes and fix street lights."

"How will we pay for trash collections?" others said. "Our streets will stink of rotting litter. We'll be overrun with rats."

"Perhaps it's time to vote for a new mukhtar," some even said.

But the mukhtar merely smiled and nodded. "Just you wait and see," he said.

And we did wait. And we did see.

ISIS attacked the city every day for months. Even now that the Kurdish People's Protection Units have pushed them back, the fighting goes on endlessly and US airstrikes can happen at any time. Every power station in Kobani has been destroyed and most of the utility poles are smashed in half, tossed like broken logs along the roads. When the overhead lines were first dragged down by explosions, the cables sparked and whipped like live snakes but the current soon ran out. Now Alan and his friends drag the dead cables behind them as they play soldiers.

The mukhtar opened his stores to hand out a generator and diesel drum to every inner courtyard in our district. Now the families still living here are full of praise for his farsighted thinking.

"What a great investment," some say. "ISIS might be here for a long time but we have power to cook our food and light our nights."

"How else would we manage to feed our families? To brighten the dark?" others say.

"We're lucky to have such a smart mukhtar," everyone says.

In the early evening, the streets in our neighborhood vibrate with the engines of the generators. Blue diesel smoke fills the air as women gather to cook eggplant and canned tomatoes and rice. My family joins in the bright light and buzzing energy. Once the food is cooked, Dayah eats inside with Dapir, Bushra and the other women and girls. They talk about who has left the neighborhood, or the latest school or health clinic to explode. Babies and toddlers doze in their laps or play around their feet.

In the courtyard, the men and boys eat under the stars. If my father gets home on time from his pharmacy, he joins their talk of the war, or of having no jobs, or when might be the right time to join family in Canada and Turkey and Germany. Alan and the little kids run around, pretending to shoot each other.

"This is boring," Hamza says tonight.

We sneak down the road to sit on the crumbling wall of the mukhtar's mother's house. She lived there until six weeks ago when a barrel bomb tossed from a helicopter smashed into it. Luckily for her, she was visiting her daughter and grandchildren on the other side of Kobani at the time. The front wall was blown out, but by some freaky coincidence, her carved wooden dresser full of her antique china collection was left perfectly intact. She took herself and her china collection to live with her daughter.

"Bring the women's shoes and phones over to my house in the morning," Hamza says. "The buyer will collect them at lunchtime." The light from the courtyard shines on his face.

"I've only got two pairs of shoes left," I say. "One pair got left behind after the airstrike."

"Are you serious?" Hamza says. "What am I supposed to tell the buyer?"

"Give him something else," I say. "An extra phone or one of the shirts."

"You're not being professional, Ghalib. We supply to order. We don't offer random substitutes like phones and shirts. How do you think I secured our buyer in the first place? This is not a smash-and-grab business."

Hamza looks at me. Something in his expression makes my scalp tingle. "We have to go back for a third pair, Ghalib."

"I'm going to the souq with Dayah and Bushra in the morning."

"The buyer comes at lunchtime."

"You'll have to go on your own."

"You're the one who lost the shoes, Ghalib."

"I didn't *lose* them," I say. "They were collateral damage."

"It was your fault."

"We had no choice," I say. "We had to get home."

"There's always a choice, Ghalib," Hamza says. "I choose to go to the souq and get another pair." He smiles as he looks at me. "Tonight."

"*What?* Don't be crazy, Hamza. Nobody goes to Freedom Square at night."

"It's early."

"It's dark."

"Scared, Ghalib?" His sneer is unmistakable.

"There are unexploded shells. And snipers. And ISIS. Not to mention Protection Units every-where—they're not going to just let us get away with snatching stuff."

"Everyone knows where the sleeping bombs are," Hamza says. "ISIS and the Protection Units won't be out until later. We'll be back by then."

"*We?*" I say. "You think I'm going too?"

Hamza jumps off the wall. He brushes dust from his trousers. Peers into the courtyard where knots of people eat and talk in the blue smoke. Soft voices reach across the night. The smell of cooking hangs in the air.

"Of course you'll come, Ghalib," Hamza says. "We're family."

I blink. I look at Hamza. He's far braver, far stronger than me. It's his job to make decisions; it's my job to go along with them, even if I don't want to.

"What will I tell Baba and Dayah?" I say.

"Nothing! We'll be back before they even notice. It'll take less than an hour."

We skirt the bright courtyards around the mosque, avoiding any light that might expose us. At first it's easy to see, but as soon as we move away from our neighborhood, everything melts into inky blackness. Familiar streets are unrecognizable from a couple of years ago, the ruined houses empty and silent. Hardly anybody lives here now. Only a few places have candlelight gleaming through scorched curtains or open doorways. Rubble heaps are the remains of friends' houses, of the corner shop where we bought ice cream, of our local bakery. Walking here in the daytime is bad enough, but at night, ghosts of the dead haunt these deserted streets. I spook at every sound: rats cheeping in the trash, broken bricks settling in the night. My heart skips a beat when I see the glow of a cigarette tip burning in the dark. A man stands silently, watching us pass.

"We'll go along Aleppo Way," Hamza says. His voice is loud in the darkness. "It's quicker at this time. Not so much rubble and masonry."

"But lots of Protection Units," I add.

"They won't touch us."

The streets reek more at night: darkness draws out the smells. I hold my breath as the stench of rotting trash mixes with smoke and pulverized concrete, smashed-up sewers and rot. We reach the unexploded bomb half-buried in the ground at the start of Aleppo Way, its nose buried deep in the dirt, wing blades pointing at the sky. We've passed it dozens of times, daring each other to touch it, but the night bloats its evil. I scrunch my fists in my pockets and sneak by, not wanting to brush my fingertips against it. Even Hamza is silent and swift as he sidles past. We pause to stare the length of Aleppo Way— the longest stretch of our journey. Light from cooking fires in derelict buildings softens the dense dark.

"So many fires," I say.

They could be fires of the Protection Units, or of local people forced out of their homes. They could even be the fires of ISIS troops sneaking back into the city, creeping close to our neighborhood.

"Protection Units, Ghalib," Hamza assures me. "They're not the enemy."

He strides down Aleppo Way, passing the scorched skeletons of trees along the street. Glass crunches close to me as I catch up with him. I lurch against Hamza. He shoves me away.

"You're worse than Alan," he says.

But a thread of nervousness weaves through his laughter. It dies completely when a man steps from a broken building. I see his silhouette. The silhouette of his raised gun. My heart hammers. Words spill out of me, stuttered, broken.

"We're locals!" I say. I lift my arms over my head. "We're locals! No weapons. No gun." My voice cracks.

The man stops dead. He looks us up and down. He holds his gun steady. "What are you doing here?" he says.

Firelight shines behind him. I can't see his face: only his silhouette. Beside me, the brave and mighty Hamza has clammed up. I look at him to answer, and my heart stops as he slinks behind me. *Me*—his younger cousin!

"What are you doing here?" the man says again.

"Women's shoes," I blurt out. "We're looking for women's shoes." It sounds ridiculous. What will he think?

He lowers the gun. Pulls hard on his cigarette. "Not easy to walk in women's shoes over rubble, boys."

His voice is louder than necessary. To draw the attention of others inside, I realize, as four men emerge from the broken building.

Their uniforms show they're with the Protection Units, not ISIS. They won't shoot us, but we might get a beating. The men circle us. They can hardly see Hamza because my swaggering cousin has shrunk to almost nothing behind me. The first man teases us for the amusement of his friends even though he must see my terror. Now that he has an audience, he puts on a silly voice, high and girlish.

"Will you bring me back a new headscarf?" he says. The others laugh.

"Let them go, Mahmoud," one of them says. "They're only kids."

"They shouldn't be out looking for women's shoes at night," Mahmoud says. He looks at me. Even though it's dark, even though his face is in shadow, it seems that his eyes glow with red fire like the tip of his smoldering cigarette. His gaze burns into me.

"You know a war rages in the city, boy? You know you could be shot dead at any time?"

I can't bring myself to say it was Hamza's stupid idea. That I didn't want to come in the first place. That I agree with Mahmoud. All I can do is nod dumbly and wish I was anywhere but here.

"Do your parents know where you are?" Mahmoud says.

"No."

"Then get back to them before I march you home and shame you in front of your father. You and that cowardly boy behind you."

This is the truest thing Mahmoud has said. I stumble around and crash straight into Hamza, huddled behind me. I put my hands on his shoulders and turn him from the men. I hiss in his ear, my rising laughter clear to him.

"Come on, cowardly boy."

I get no further. A deafening roar engulfs the dark city streets. A wavering beam of light snaps on high in the night sky. Powerful and glaring, it shreds the darkness. Someone screams.

"Chopper!" one of the soldiers says.

I spin back, stunned by the sudden noise and light. In the dazzle, Mahmoud points skyward.

"Barrel bomb!"

He races from the blaze of brightness and the deafening racket.

The roar of the chopper shrieks loud and low until I think it will tear my head off. Its beam slashes glaring light through the blackness. Violent gusts blast my ears and face. Clamor and chaos slice my blood and heartbeat.

Men raise their guns. Blast them skyward in a blaze of fire and bullets. Tearing wind beats me to the ground. Hamza screams. He is still screaming when I shove him into the broken building.

3

I push myself up from the smoking rubble. Wipe dust and pulverized plaster from my eyes and nose. My throat stings. I spit grit. My lungs scald in the burning air. The chopper is gone, taking with it the searing light and thunderous throb.

I look around from where I sit on top of hot rubble and broken brick. It shifts and slides beneath me with the sound of broken crockery. Everything has changed. Everything is different from moments before. Everywhere reeks of hot metal and burning fuel. Teetering walls grind and strain. My back and shoulders throb from bricks and chunks of plaster that beat me as they crashed down. My fingers find tender lumps on my skull but no blood. No broken bones. I clamber to my feet, seeking something to steady me. I reach for half-walls and broken pillars.

The ground slides and tilts and burns my feet. My shoes are gone, blasted off in the explosion.

"Hamza?"

My voice is small and broken. Thick with dust. I cough. Spit again. I search for Hamza in the darkness and smoke and dust. He must be close by. But my world has shifted.

The whole building has shifted. The blast and the collapse and the chaos could have flung him anywhere. Close to me, a broken body lies under a heap of smoking rubble. Scraps of burnt uniform flutter in the rising heat. It's one of the men who stood next to me moments ago. Some of him is missing. There's a lot of blood. I look away.

I clamber through the hot night. Feeling. Searching. Rocks and blown-out bricks tumble and clatter. A terrible grinding creaks up high, as though the whole structure might collapse at any moment. I need to get out. But I also need to find Hamza.

Fires hiss in corners, seeking something to devour. They flare high and angry as wooden doors and old curtains catch light. They give a little brightness in the ash-thick air. Heat rises with the oily smoke.

I see another figure. I'm afraid to look, but I have to know. I slide and scramble over the hot uneven ground. Hamza!

I crouch next to where he's sprawled on his back, blasted among the charred debris. He doesn't move. He might be dead. His legs are wedged between broken bricks and fallen walls. One arm is flung above his head, the other across his chest. I wipe ash and grit from his face. Scoop dirt and broken bits from his mouth with my finger. Something hot and wet slicks over his face. I think it's blood. I think the sharp broken bits are teeth, but there's not enough light to see. I lean close and listen. Hamza breathes, but it's ragged and unsteady. I clear the rubble across his chest so he can get air, even though that air is thick with smoke and ash and fumes. My body shakes. My head pounds. We have to get out.

I grab Hamza's dead-weight arms. He gasps and moans. I drag him up. Slowly, he slumps to half-sitting. Broken stones roll from him. I squat low and hook my hands beneath his armpits.

"Get moving, Hamza," I say. "Coming here was your *stupid* idea. Getting out is my brilliant one."

I rock him forward, haul him back. Somehow it works. Slowly, he eases from the rubble. My back aches. Sweat runs down my face. But I don't stop. The flames from the fires rise higher. The smoke is thick and black. Something hisses deep in the building's belly as though a massive snake is about to strike. The groaning up high has ceased. Now, there is only silence from the remaining walls and dangling roof. That scares me more. The building has drawn into itself. Brooding.

I see a black oblong shape through the heat-shimmer: an open doorway that might lead out. Hamza's legs give occasional lurches, strange spasms that ease his dead weight in my arms. And *Alhamdulillah*, they help propel him toward the open doorway. As we get closer, I hear men's voices. Shouting. Distant alarms. We are no longer alone. I'm exhausted, but I'm nearly there.

"They're here," a man says.

There is shouting. Running feet. "Grab them."

"It's about to come down."

Hamza's weight is lifted from me. Someone scoops me into his arms. I'm carried swiftly across the dark street and into another building. Hissing fires and oily smells fade. I'm propped against a wall. Two men lay Hamza next to me. One of them is Mahmoud. He spins around as the ground shudders and rumbles.

"There it goes!" he says.

The building collapses in a rush of fire and thunder. Scalding ash storms across to engulf me again. I scream and cover my head. I am certain I will die.

"You're safe," Mahmoud says. He puts his hand on my shoulder. "I'll stay with you."

"I want Dayah," I say. I sound like Alan.

He hands me a bottle of water. I drink it down, gulping, retching. "Slowly," he says. "You'll make yourself sick."

After the collapse, silence rushes in as always. We all hold our breath. The night waits. We can't go out until the streets are safe: there could be more explosions. More barrel bombs from the chopper. I slump against the wall. I can't think straight. Hurt is all through me: my head, my body, my thoughts. Darkness swells in my blood as though great black wings beat inside me and above me. Every breath is fire in my lungs.

The men fret around Hamza. He doesn't move. There are urgent whispers. Mahmoud squats next to me.

"Who is your friend?" he says.

"Hamza," I say. "He's my cousin." My breathing bubbles and rattles.

"Where do you live?"

I whisper my street, my district. My family name. It hurts to speak. Mahmoud leans close to hear.

"Is Hamza dead?" I say. My throat gurgles.

"No," Mahmoud says. "Rest now. I'll get your father." He slips out.

I lean back. Close my eyes. Hamza is going to die. I should have refused to go downtown with him. I should have told my parents. Dayah always says Hamza is foolish. Even though I'm younger, she says I'm the sensible one. I was not sensible this time. I should have stopped him.

After a long time, Mahmoud returns with Baba and Uncle Yousef. Baba throws aside his bag of medicines. He kneels beside me. Snatches me into his arms. I gasp and wheeze and cry at the same time. My lungs have no breath in them.

"My son," Baba says.

"I'm sorry, Baba," I say. "I'm sorry."

My words are lost in tears and rattling breath and Baba's shoulder. He holds me tight.

"Don't speak," he says. "We'll get you home. We'll make you better."

Baba, Uncle Yousef, and Mahmoud carry us home by torchlight. It's a long journey with a great deal of shouting, shifting and moving through rubble and broken streets. I'm terrified of more barrel bombs. More explosions.

"Baba," I say.

"I'm here," he says.

"I'll stay with you," he says.

"Breathe slowly," he says.

I bury my face in his chest. Gasp for air. I hurt all over.

They take us to Baba's pharmacy. The lights shudder and tremble from the generator. The smell of diesel is comforting. A nurse who used to work in the hospital before it was bombed has made up camp beds for us. There are medicines and bandages. Baba unrolls tubing from the oxygen tank. He attaches it to a little flask with breathing medicine and straps a mask on my face.

"It will help," he says. "Breathe slowly."

Dayah is there too. She squats in front of me.

"I'm sorry," I say. Tears run down my cheeks.

"Hush now," she says. She strokes my face.

"Is Hamza dead?" I say.

"No. You saved his life."

Gently, carefully, she peels scorched and smoking cloth from my raw skin. Grazes and burns cover my body. Dayah fills a little basin with warm water to wash my arms and legs. She combs filth from my hair. She examines each wound closely. She mutters. She tuts. When she touches my blackened feet, I scream. What I thought was dirt turns out to be charred blisters. Hot bricks and rubble have burned my skin. Baba sets up an IV with painkillers, but even so, I cry out and grip Dayah when he cleans and bandages my feet.

"You'll need to stay here tonight," Baba says.

I don't want to sleep in the pharmacy, with its bright lights and noisy generator. There could be more barrel bombs. More explosions. I want to be in my own bed. I want to be home with Baba and Dayah and Dapir. With Bushra and Alan.

"I want to go home."

"Your lungs and feet are burned, Ghalib," Baba says. "There are medicines here to treat your breathing and pain."

"Please, Baba," I beg. "I want to go home."

"I want him home," Dayah says. "I can care for him."

While Hamza lies unconscious on the camp bed with the nurse hovering around him, Baba carries me through the dark streets. I grip him tightly and try not to cry out when he stumbles over broken bricks. Dayah carries my IV and medicines.

Baba lays me gently on the sofa in the front room. Alan and Bushra sleep in the back room but Dapir is awake and waiting for us. She helps to arrange my bedding, to make me comfortable, to fuss and care for me.

"My brave grandson," she says. "You saved your cousin's life."

Dayah sits on the edge of the sofa. "We can't stay in Kobani." Her voice is brittle. "Not after today."

I pull the breathing mask from my face. "I'm not leaving."

"This is no place to live, Ghalib," Dayah says.

"I'm staying with Hamza." I wheeze and gasp. Replace my mask to suck oxygen into my burning lungs.

"Stop speaking," Baba says. He adjusts the flow of oxygen. "Calm down and breathe slowly."

"It was my fault." I struggle for air. "I can't leave him."

"We have to leave," Dayah says to Baba. "Please!" Her voice is a whisper. "For our children."

Baba says nothing. The quiet, broken only by my wheezing, reminds me of the brooding in the burning building before it crashed down. I wait for the rush of fire and thunder from Baba, but it doesn't come. His voice is soft when he finally speaks.

"I have work to do here," Baba says. "We have no choice."

Hamza's words from earlier flash into my head: *There's always a choice, Ghalib.* I understand the wisdom of those words now. We make choices all the time. I chose badly tonight. I'm the sensible one, yet I was foolish enough to follow him into the city. I should have stopped him. Dayah's words cut through my thinking.

"No choice?" She raises her voice. "No *choice?* We can choose to leave, like almost everyone else. We can't stay in this place of death."

"Who will look after my patients?" Baba says. "Every hospital and clinic is blown up."

"Who will look after your *family?*" Dayah says. "They come first. Look at Ghalib—he almost got killed today. Hamza is critically injured. They took Alan to the souq during an airstrike. We can't go on like this. *I* can't go on like this."

A sob breaks Dayah's words. She puts her head in her hands. Dapir sits next to her, stroking her back.

"I'm sorry, Dayah," I say again. My heart thumps hard. I breathe slowly. Take in clean air before I speak again. Everything that happened today is my fault. "I should have stopped Hamza." I breathe.

"You saved his life," Dayah says.

"I nearly killed him," I say. *Breathe.* "If it wasn't for the Protection Units"—*breathe*—"we would be dead now."

"Don't say that," says Dapir. "Hamza is alive because of you! And Alhamdulillah, you too survived."

"If we leave," Baba says, "where would Kurdish families go for medical care? My pharmacy is all that remains."

"Kurdish families are not your responsibility," Dayah says. Her voice is steady now, only a little above a whisper. Sadness puddles all through her words. "There are aid agencies and foreign clinics to care for them."

"They don't understand Kurdish traditions," Baba says. "They don't even speak our language. How can they provide for my patients?"

"How can I provide for my children?" Dayah says. "Food is running out. We line up for hours for clean water. There are no schools. Alan hasn't had physical therapy in months. And today, two of them almost died!"

Now Baba sits with his head in his hands. I understand the battle in his heart, but before I take in enough air to lift my words, Dapir speaks to Dayah.

"This is home for us, Gardina," she says. "Syrian Kurds are our people. My son can't desert them now."

"I'm staying," I say.

Baba checks the breathing medicine in the little flask. He touches the bandages on my feet lightly.

"You need to rest," he says. He turns to Dayah. "We'll talk about this tomorrow. It's too late now."

"It might be too late tomorrow," Dayah says.

In spite of being in my own home with my family, I can't sleep. My heart is scarred by raw terror. Heavy with remorse. Frightened Hamza will die. My blood darkens in a way I have never known before. When I close my eyes, the chopper slices and throbs in my skull. Fire and smoke fill my nose. Grit and burning ash grate in my teeth. I search for Hamza in the burning rubble, crying out for him. Twice in the night, Baba holds me when my nightmares shudder me from sleep. My breathing bubbles and gurgles.

"I'm here," he says.

"Breathe easy," he says.

"You're safe," he says.

The overseas aid clinic sends medics to examine Hamza and me.

"We need to take Ghalib to the pharmacy for the doctors," Baba says.

"I'm not moving him," Dayah says. "Let them come here."

"They're foreign doctors! They don't come to people's houses."

"They can come to this one. He is mine and he will stay with me."

After they examine Hamza, the foreign medics with their interpreter come to our home. Right into my room. Dayah puts on a new scarf. She tries to make Bushra wear one.

"I don't need one," Bushra says. "I'm at home."

"It's respectful," Dayah says.

People gather to watch the medics arrive. Even the mukhtar wants to meet them. The doctor examines my feet and my other cuts and burns. She helps me to sit up so she can listen to my breathing. She looks at the medicines Baba has given me. She checks that we have clean water from the water truck. The interpreter translates her words into Arabic. He doesn't speak Kurdish.

"What's going to happen?" Bushra says after they've left.

"Are they going to take Ghalib away?" Alan says.

"I'm not going with foreigners," I say.

Later, when Baba returns from the pharmacy, he says, "They're taking Hamza to the foreign aid clinic."

I look away from him. I don't know what to say. All I can think is that I should have stopped us from going into the Freedom Square.

I feel Dayah's hand on my shoulder. "We'll pray for his recovery," she says. Her touch gives me strength.

"I'm not going to the clinic, Baba," I say.

"You will stay here," Baba says. "They've given me stronger medicine to help your breathing. And fresh dressings for your feet."

"And Hamza?" I say.

"He'll get proper care and the right medicines," Baba says.

4

"Bushra, we need fresh water," Dapir says. "The container is empty."

"Why is it always 'Bushra, we need this'? 'Bushra, we need that'?" my sister says. "Am I the only one in this house?" She snatches up the container and gives me one of her looks.

"Don't look at me!" I say. "I can't walk to the water truck."

"Ghalib's legs don't work right," Alan says. "He's like me."

"Go on now, Bushra," Dayah says. "Take Alan with you."

They head off to the nearest army truck where Protection Units supply fresh water from huge drums. I sit on the sofa in the front room to look out at the street through the open door. I don't need my oxygen mask or breathing medicine anymore. My lungs are clear when I rest, but if I get out of breath, my chest rattles and burns. My feet are still bandaged and though I can't walk properly outside, I hobble around the house.

As for Hamza, there has been little change in his condition since the night of the barrel bomb. He needs a lot of medical care. His parents are the only ones allowed to visit. They return with worried faces to talk to my parents in hushed whispers. They throw concerned glances at me. Baba doesn't tell me much, but I know Hamza might still die.

When Alan and Bushra return two hours later, Protection Unit soldiers are with them. They carry the water keg.

"Soldiers!" I say. "Soldiers are coming."

Soldiers visiting a house never bring good news. This can only mean trouble. Dayah and Dapir rush to the door.

"That's my cousin Dima," Dayah says.

Dima greets us as she comes into our front room; Mahmoud is with her.

"So here is the boy who searches for women's shoes at night," Mahmoud says. He can't resist teasing me.

"Mahmoud tells me you were brave. That you saved Hamza's life," Dima says.

"I wasn't brave," I say. "He's my cousin."

She looks different from how I remember her, dressed in her soldier's uniform and heavy army boots, her long dark hair swept back under an olive-colored headscarf. I'm a little nervous of the rifle swinging from her shoulder, the row of bullets hanging around her neck. The smell of dust and sweat and hard work rises from her as she leans over to look at my bandaged feet.

"We need soldiers like you," Mahmoud says. "When you're better, you will join the Protection Units to fight ISIS and pro-government forces."

These are dangerous words. I stare at Mahmoud and Dima. I stare at my mother, who stands at the open door with her hand to her mouth. It looks as though every drop of blood drains from my face.

"I'm thirteen," I say at last. "Too young to fight. The army won't accept me."

"You're strong and brave," Mahmoud says. "That's enough."

"You too, Bushra," Dima says. "You will join with Ghalib. We need new recruits. Fresh young blood to continue the fight."

Even if I was old enough to join the Protection Units, I don't think I would ever fight in a war. I'm not courageous. I want to be a pharmacist like Baba. I want to help people get better. But Bushra has a brave spirit like Mahmoud and Dima. She smiles now, her face flushed pink. She holds her head high and looks Dima in the eye.

After Dima and Mahmoud leave, Bushra and I look at Dayah and Dapir. They have many words in their eyes, but we say nothing in front of Alan. The first opportunity we get to talk is later that evening when Alan is in bed and Baba is home.

"Mahmoud and Dima expect Ghalib and Bushra to fight," Dayah says. Her voice trembles.

"My children will not fight in the war," Baba says.

"The Protection Units will not accept a refusal," Dayah says.

"But Dima is family," I say. "Does that mean nothing to her?"

"The war is in her heart and blood, Ghalib," Dayah says. "Family comes second."

"I'm not afraid of fighting," Bushra says.

"You are not fighting, Bushra," Baba says.

"They need new soldiers, Baba. I can fight like Dima. I'm almost sixteen."

"You are fifteen," Baba says. "Neither of you will fight. That is my final word."

I'm relieved to hear Baba's final word, but Bushra sets her mouth in that sour way of hers.

"I dreamed of being an engineer," she says. "Then the war blew up my school and killed my friends. My dreams are dead, Baba. I'm not afraid to fight ISIS."

Silence falls. I stare at Bushra. I've never heard anything so sad. So final. So brave.

"Family might come second for Dima," I say. "But family comes first for me. This war isn't in *my* heart and blood. I want to be a pharmacist, not a soldier. And Bushra wants to be an engineer."

"Or a soldier," Bushra says.

"But an engineer first."

"Maybe," she says. She's not making this easy for me.

"I don't want to leave Kobani," I say. "I want to go to the souq with Hamza again. I want to go to university. To open my own Kurdish pharmacy. But I'm afraid, Baba. I'm afraid to be a soldier." I swallow.

Baba sits in his chair by the open doorway, facing the dark street. I can't see his expression, but I know he is listening.

"Baba, when there's nothing left for us here except death, then surely it must be time to leave?"

When Baba speaks, his voice is little more than a whisper. "You're right, Ghalib."

Bushra gasps—a soft intake of breath. Dayah speaks, and her words hold so much hope, so much brightness, they ache my heart.

"It's time to leave Syria?" she says.

Baba turns his gaze to rest on me. Tears glint in his eyes. "Your words twist a knife in my heart, Ghalib. I have to listen to them. I have to hear my family."

He looks at Dayah and Bushra. They hold each other, eyes bright with hope.

"We will leave Syria and travel somewhere safe," he says. "But our leaving must be a secret. Nobody can know, in case anyone in the Protection Units hears about it. Not the neighbors. Not the mukhtar. Not even Alan. It would put us all in danger."

"What about Hamza?" I say.

"Hamza and his parents must stay until he's well enough to travel," Baba says.

– – –

Everything changes from that day on. Even though we know this is something we need to do, that doesn't make it any easier. Every day, something is

41

packed away or goes missing. Every day, a full feeling in my chest seems a little closer to brimming over. Today the glass-fronted bookshelves are empty. All of Baba's old pharmacy books, our books of Kurdish poetry. Gone.

"Where are they?" I say.

"Packed away," Dayah says.

"We're leaving them?"

"We can't bring books with us."

"They were always with us," I say. "And now they won't be."

"You never even looked at them," Bushra says.

"That's not the point. They were here if I *wanted* to look at them. Now they won't be."

"There are other books to read," Dayah says.

"He never reads," Bushra says. "Unless it's soccer results."

"Baba might want to read them," I say. "He sometimes reads Kurdish epic poems."

"Not for a long time," Dayah says.

"Clearly it will be a long time again," I say.

We have to work hard to keep the secret from Alan. He's smart. He knows something is going on and tries his best to find out. Every time I turn around, I nearly trip over him.

"You're being weird again, Alan," I say.

"You're hiding something," he says.

"Go and find someone else to be weird with."

"There's no one."

"Annoy Bushra."

"She told me to annoy *you*."

"Does Dayah know you're sucking your thumb again?"

He pulls his hand from his mouth and looks at his chapped thumb.

In the front room, Dayah and Bushra fold up the embroidered rugs and beautiful wall hangings, the floor cushions and curtains. Stacked on the table, their colorful stripes and woven designs folded inside, they make the rest of the room feel cold and empty. Alan stares at the ghostly squares left behind by the rich tapestries on the walls.

"Why did you take them down?" he says.

"Too much dust and smoke in the air," Dayah says.

"You never took them down before."

"Then it is well past time to take them down."

"The walls look horrible," Alan says.

"But the hangings will be clean," Bushra says.

"I don't like it."

"Ghalib is going to get his bandages changed," Bushra says. "Keep him company, Alan."

Baba changes the dressings on my feet every other day. He cleans the oozing blisters, examines them for infection. It hurts so much that I grip the seat and bite the inside of my mouth. Baba talks to me the whole time. He always has something to tell me, a story or a memory from his childhood, to distract me. It rarely works.

"I have savings put aside," he says today. He smears on cooling antiseptic cream with his fingertips. "For university education for the three of you. For Bushra's dowry. For surgery on Alan's leg."

"My leg doesn't want surgery," Alan says. He holds the tub of cream.

Baba studies my feet. "You're healing well."

They look like lumps of barbecued meat. "They hurt so much."

Alan leans over to see. I look away. I don't want to see them. I try to concentrate on Baba's words.

"It's invested in my pharmacy, in gold and orchards," Baba says.

"What is?"

"My savings," Baba says. "I've thought a lot about it."

This is more than random chat to distract me. I listen closely.

"Education and marriage and medical treatment are secondary now, Ghalib," Baba says. "Other things take priority. Some of my investments will go toward those other things now."

He looks at me. I see many meanings in his eyes, but he talks in code because Alan hangs on every word. He looks from Baba to me and back again, trying to figure out the conversation.

Baba means his investments will pay for our way out of Syria. I listen so closely that he finishes cleaning my burns and I hardly notice the pain. He stands straight. Cracks his back. He wraps my feet in clean dressings, which make them feel secure. His words also make *me* feel secure, knowing he has a plan to get us to safety.

"What are you talking about, Baba?" Alan says.

"Your future," Baba says. "All of our futures. When the war is over, there will still be money left in my orchards and my pharmacy—provided they're not blown up."

Something about getting ready to leave fills me up in a way I can't explain. I say nothing to Dapir or Dayah, and certainly not to Bushra. The only time I let my feelings out is when I lie in bed at night and listen to the distant *krump* of explosions and barrel bombs, to the alarms and sirens after an airstrike. I smell the fires. See their glow stain the clouds. Everything wells up inside me then. I am scared it will spill out. My blood thickens and darkens. I don't know what frightens me most: staying in Kobani with airstrikes and barrel bombs and the threat of Mahmoud and Dima, or leaving Hamza and everything I love to go somewhere unknown and different.

Baba knows how I feel. We don't talk about it, but sometimes he sits on my bed when everyone else is asleep. We watch the fire-shadows dance on the ceiling. We listen to distant explosions. Baba says if we lie as still as dead people, perhaps our fears will be still too and let us sleep. We don't talk unless my nightmares are so bad that he is already beside me when I wake up. Then he holds me tight. He stays until I am calm. Until the darkness in my blood softens and fades.

"I'm here," he says.

"Breathe slowly," he says.

Sometimes he stays until the next morning, in case I have nightmares again.

5

The night before we leave, I sit on the floor in the back room to sort what I will bring with me. Alan stretches out on his cot to watch.

"What are you doing?" he says.

"Sorting."

"Why?"

"Because."

"Because what?"

"Just because."

I make three piles: Essentials, Maybes and Definitely Nots. Essentials include my computer games, my music player and headphones, my three favorite books (about soccer, survival in the wild, and spies), the Syrian soccer team strip and boots I got for my birthday, my sports watch and my pocketknife. I add my leather wallet and best sports medals from the last two years in school.

My Definitely Nots include my schoolbooks, jacket, sweaters and jeans I don't like, action toys, board games and old sports cards. Alan snatches up one of my old medals.

"Are you giving this away?"

"Maybe."

"Can I have it?" He turns the imitation gold medal over.

"If you like."

"Thanks!"

My Maybes pile is tiny: deodorant and body spray from Dayah, and a book from Bushra that I was going to put in the Definitely Nots, but she might see it there.

Dayah comes in. "How's it going?"

I point to the Definitely Nots. "I'm leaving these behind."

Alan looks from Dayah to me. He sits up.

Dayah points to the Essentials. "And these?"

"They're coming."

"They certainly are not."

I look at her. I look at my Essentials. "I need everything here."

"Sports medals? Computer games?"

"Essential," I say.

"Are we going somewhere?" Alan says.

Bushra noses in with a smirk on her face. "Where do you think we're going to put all that, Ghalib?"

"*We* don't need to put it anywhere," I say. "I'll carry my own stuff in my own sports bag."

Dayah takes up my quilted jacket. "You'll need this."

She lifts my schoolbooks, my sweaters, and old jeans from Definitely Nots. "And these."

"I don't want them."

"Where are we going?" Alan says.

"You'll need warm clothes, Ghalib," Dayah says. "And schoolbooks."

"I don't have room."

"Then take out the games and toys."

"They are *not* games and toys," I say. "They are essential items. *Survival* items. It's murder in the schoolyard, Dayah. It'll be worse in foreign lands. I can't survive without this stuff."

"Don't be dramatic," Dayah says.

Bushra reaches down to add my deodorant and body spray to the Essentials pile. "I'm not going with you if you don't have these. Where's your toothbrush?"

Alan stands on his cot now. "We're leaving Kobani!" he says. "That's why Ghalib is packing."

"You said I could decide what to bring," I say to Dayah, ignoring Alan. "Now you and Bushra are making all the decisions. It's nothing to do with her. I'm supposed to be making my *own* choices. I'm supposed to be growing up."

Alan's face is shining. "I'm right, aren't I?"

"Two words, Ghalib," Bushra says. "*Bare. Essentials.* Which one do you not understand?"

"Four words, Bushra," I say. "*Mind. Your. Own. Business.*"

"That's enough," Dayah says. "Go into the front room, Bushra."

Alan jumps up and down on his cot and nearly falls off. "We're really leaving!"

Dayah lifts him down. "Go with Bushra. She'll tell you what's going on."

When they've gone, she turns back to me. "We have to carry everything, Ghalib. There's no room for luxuries."

"These aren't luxuries. You're making me take stuff I don't even want. Sweaters and a jacket, stupid old schoolbooks."

"Either you decide what to leave behind, or

I decide for you. You can't bring everything and that's final."

"It sounds like you've already made the decisions," I say. "Without even listening to what I want."

———

It's still dark when Dapir wakes me. We leave Kobani today. "Stay quiet," she says. "Alan is still asleep."

I sit up. My belly is sick. Alan doesn't move as I pull on my jeans and sandals. The house is quiet but busy. Dapir and Dayah are wrapping food parcels in the front room. Bushra is piling bags and bedrolls at the front door.

"Help Dapir to make breakfast," Dayah says to me.

"I don't want anything to eat."

"You're not leaving this house without a proper breakfast," Dayah says. "Bushra, wake Alan and strip the beds."

After a breakfast none of us enjoys, Baba cleans and binds my feet, while Dapir and Dayah empty the cabinets of food and Bushra gets Alan ready. Baba goes up to the attic and brings down a strongbox full of gold jewelry I've never seen before: heavy necklaces and chains, watches and rings. Alan, Bushra and I stare as he carefully lifts each item. He gives five gold necklaces, two rings, and a bracelet to Dayah, a necklace and gold bangle to Bushra. Dapir doesn't want gold. "I'm too old to be weighed down with jewelry," she says.

Baba clasps a gold wrist chain and neck chain on me, and even Alan wears a fine gold chain.

"Keep them safe," Baba says. "These are our tickets to a new life."

I finger the heavy gold and wonder how far it will take us. Our nearest border crossing is in Mursitpinar, twenty minutes' drive from Kobani, but Turkey closed down the border there months ago, after the Protection Units took back Kobani from ISIS. Before the war, Dapir, Dayah and Aunt Najah crossed at Mursitpinar on day trips to Turkey. They came home with gifts: jeans or a wallet for me, a new skirt for Bushra, Turkish delight and embroidered cloths.

"Now we have to travel to Aleppo," Baba says. "From there, to the crossing at Bab al-Hawa."

Only Aunt Najah and Uncle Yousef come to see us off. No one else knows our secret. Dapir and Dayah hug them tightly. Bushra clings to Aunt Najah.

"Give our blessings and apologies to the mukhtar," Baba says.

"He'll understand," Uncle Yousef says.

Baba gives Uncle Yousef the keys to our home. "As soon as Hamza is able to travel—"

"We will join you," Uncle Yousef says.

There are tears and broken words and kisses. Dayah sends her blessings to Hamza. I want to be gone. Saying good-bye is too difficult. Alan stays close to me, nuzzling my shirt as Aunt Najah holds me close.

"Hamza will miss you," she says.

I think of Hamza in his hospital bed in the foreign clinic.

I wonder if he even knows I'm leaving.

When the minibus arrives, it's already almost full. The bus attendant ties our luggage on the roof rack and we cram inside, finding corners and seat edges to perch on. With scarcely time for a final glance at our home, and at Uncle Yousef and Aunt Najah shuffling in the chill gray dawn, we drive off, crunching over rubble and broken brick. The sick feeling rises in my throat.

The route out of the city is bumpy and winding, especially as the driver takes sudden turns to avoid broken buildings or unknown groups clustered on the road.

"Better to avoid trouble," he says. "I don't know who they are."

"What route are you taking?" Baba says.

"Avoiding the souq," the driver says. "Missiles hit the theater last night—it's blocking the highway."

The sun is already peeking above the horizon when we finally reach the main road out of Kobani, busy with shared taxis, minibuses, and people on foot, all departing the city. The traffic slows and eventually stops. Horns blare. Men shout. I stare out at people who look as though they've already traveled a long way. Everyone carries packs and bags and string-tied parcels. Kurds in bright clothing. Groups of men with long beards and loud voices. Women in the all-enveloping black garments ISIS makes them wear. Nothing of them can be seen— their faces and bodies hidden entirely, hands and feet covered with black gloves and socks. They walk behind their husbands and sons. Bushra watches them with a troubled look.

"What's the delay?" she says.

"Road block," the driver says.

"Who controls it?" says a man in the back seat.

"Protection Units—who else?" the driver says. "They'll likely search the bus."

"What are they looking for?"

"Suicide bombers. Deserters."

A glance passes between Baba and Dayah. It sends a chill up my spine. I know what they're thinking: what if Dima or Mahmoud is at the road block? What if they see us leaving the city? Darkness seeps into my blood. My grip on Alan tightens until he wriggles and looks at me.

"Has the road block been here long?" Baba says to the driver.

"Since Kurds took the city. Think it's bad getting out?" He glances at us. "Ten times worse getting back in. They're terrified ISIS or pro-government forces will take back control."

A dozen or more soldiers of the Protection Units police the roadblock. They wear uniforms and heavy army boots like Dima and Mahmoud. Weighed down with guns and bullets, the women have their hair scraped back under headscarves or baseball caps; the men are mostly clean-shaven. I scan their faces from the safety of the minibus but don't see anyone I recognize. Maybe fortune smiles on us this morning.

A soldier with his gun at the ready peers in when our turn comes. He studies each of us in turn before speaking to the driver.

"Destination?" he says.

"Aleppo," says the driver. "Back before sunset this evening."

"Aleppo is destroyed," the soldier says to all of us. "Rebel groups fight the Syrian army daily. Every morning brings more trouble. You're safer in Kobani."

"We're safer out of Syria," the driver says. "But that's not about to happen."

"IDs?" says the soldier.

The driver collects our papers and hands them over. The soldier flicks through them, matching them against each of us. He pauses when he comes to Baba's.

"Kurdish?" He leans down to find Baba. "Forces in Aleppo are targeting Kurds."

"My mother needs to visit her son," Baba says.

Dapir smiles and nods at the soldier, who looks at her. My heart races.

"Bring him back to Kobani," the soldier says to Dapir. "He'll be safer here with the Protection Units."

He hands back our papers. Waves us on. Nobody in the minibus says anything as we clear the road block and speed along the open road, heading for Aleppo and a nonexistent uncle. I sneak a look at Baba. He watches the road ahead, not looking at me or anybody else. My heart tightens when I think of the soldier's words: *Forces in Aleppo are targeting Kurds.*

"Who is Dapir visiting?" Alan says.

"I'll tell you later."

Our journey continues without incident. Signs of war are everywhere. A rusted and blown-out tank is pulled off the road; the scorched and shredded black flag of ISIS flutters from it. Baba points out ruins of medieval palaces and ancient forts in the hills, gutted and burned by fighting. We pass bombed factories and businesses. Near lunchtime, the traffic slows again.

"Road blocks for Aleppo," the driver says.

"Controlled by?" a man says.

"Syrian Armed Forces."

"We'll get out here," the man says.

Nobody asks questions as three men get out of the minibus. It's better not to know why people want to avoid the Syrian army. Now only one other family remains on board with us. We shuffle into vacated seats as the minibus continues over a road pockmarked with bomb craters and littered with wrecked vehicles. I stare in silence: I never thought I would see destruction worse than in Kobani.

"We won't get into the Old City," the driver says.

"As near as you can," Baba says.

"They'll divert us to the highway."

The Syrian army doesn't check papers like the Protection Units. They peer into the back of the minibus, scanning our faces, then wave us on.

"Looking for men," the driver says. "Perhaps our friends were right to get out earlier."

"We're heading west," Baba says. "Can you get us to the road out of the city?"

"Too dangerous to go that far."

"Where can we get transport west?"

The driver looks at Baba. "No minibuses. No microbuses. No shared taxis. Nothing left in Aleppo. Only transport like mine coming from Kobani or Homs—here and back in one day. Nobody will stay in Aleppo. Nobody works out of Aleppo."

A second road block diverts us to the ring road. Crowds of people hang around, sitting, waiting, walking. Others get out of buses and shared taxis to walk into the Old City. "We'll get out here," the man with the other family says.

Six of them climb out. They pay the driver and

disappear into the crowd. Only my family is left. The minibus swings onto the ring road. Traffic is backed up. We edge along slowly. After ten minutes, the driver pulls over. "End of the line. Or I won't make it back to Kobani before dark."

"We need to go farther," says Baba.

"I'm not sitting in this traffic. It could cost me my life. You'll be quicker cutting through the Old City on foot and walking out on the west road."

Dayah looks at Dapir, Alan, and me. We're not exactly candidates for long-distance walking. She questions me with her eyes. Dapir opens the door to clamber out. The bus attendant drags our luggage from the rack. Baba argues with the driver about the fare.

"I'm not paying that much!" Baba says. "You haven't even brought us where we want to go."

"I took a risk getting you here," the driver says.

Baba mutters under his breath. He settles up, and the minibus drives off. We stand alone at the side of the road, trucks and shared taxis and minibuses edging around us. I stare at the heaps of bags surrounding us. For the first time, I understand what Dayah meant when she said no room for luxuries.

6

We don't talk much as we walk. Our luggage is heavy and the day is warm. As we get closer to the Old City, we talk even less. There is too much to look at. Too much to see. Every other building is in ruins, spilling rubble and broken bricks onto the streets. Cars are rusted hulks, half buried beneath debris. I've seen similar destruction in Kobani. But here in Aleppo, it's on a much bigger scale. Whole roads are blocked with wreckage and shattered buildings. We pass through the Old City walls. In the Old City, Baba points out the fine mansions and covered souqs, the ancient caravanserais, the mosques and churches—everything burnt and broken and twisted.

And the people. I've never seen anything like the people of Aleppo. Most of the women are cloaked from head to foot in black clothing. I can't see their faces or expressions. I can't even see their hands or feet, because they wear black gloves and socks. Sometimes, I glimpse the shadow of dark eyes as they peer at us through their veils, but when they see me look, they turn away. Always in the company of male guardians who stare us down as we pass, the women whisper like black ghosts through the crumbling streets, vanishing suddenly and silently into ruined buildings. Some of them carry guns over their shoulders.

"We need to cover up more," Dayah says to Bushra and Dapir. "Before we run into religious police."

For once, my sister doesn't object. We've all heard of punishment beatings and fines in rebel-held cities for women who fail to dress a certain way. Dayah, Dapir and Bushra put on the most conservative headscarves they have. Then Dayah pins scarves across their faces so I only see their eyes. This is something they've never done in Kobani. Alan begins to cry. He butts himself against me and doesn't want to hold Dapir's hand.

"This is not the Syria I know," Dapir says.

"It's safer to cover up than to risk being punished," Dayah says.

We hurry through mostly empty, mostly silent streets. The only sound is the crunch of our feet over broken stone.

Children Alan's age don't play with pretend guns or run through the dirt dragging dead cables like in Kobani. They squat in the dust of broken door-ways instead, staring at us with big eyes and sunken cheeks. They hunt through heaps of rubble, eating what they find. They haunt the windows of dere-lict buildings, appearing like wraiths, disappearing as quickly. Their faces are yellow, their hair matted and filthy. They scratch at their bodies through torn clothing, pick at scabs on their scalps.

"What are they?" Alan says.

"Children," Baba says.

"Where are their proper clothes? Their homes?"

"They don't have any."

"Why don't foreign aid clinics help them, Baba?" I say.

"The foreign aid people have been evacuated from Aleppo," Baba says. "It's too dangerous. And local groups can only do so much."

The whole city seems to be inhabited solely by these eerie children and ghostly women. The only men we see are the male guardians with the women, and soldiers of the Syrian Armed Forces patrolling the streets in armed vehicles and trucks, guns at the ready. Always at the ready.

After a while, even looking becomes too much. I'm too full of what I see. Instead I turn my gaze to the cracked pavements. I concentrate on stepping around shattered bricks and avoiding dark stains, but still, I can't escape the familiar stench that hangs in the air like a thick fog: the sickly odor of rotting bodies and open sewers and burning. The smell clings to my nostrils and sickens my belly. There is no escape. I distract myself by guiding Alan, helping him to keep his balance on the rutted road.

At the end of a street, crowds of people gather in a square. There must be three or four hundred men, women and teenagers, their backs to us. We stop to see what's happening. The hordes are engrossed by something in their midst. It holds their rapt attention. We see flickers of movement, hear a single raised voice. A cheer goes up. The crowd begins to chant, voices rising louder and louder in unison until the sound takes over everything.

"We need to leave," Baba says.

He turns us from the crowded square. He walks fast. We scurry after him until the chanting has faded behind us. Still, Baba strides ahead. Bushra and I jog to catch up with him.

"What was that?" I say.

"Public punishments," Baba says.

"Beatings?"

"Who knows?" Baba says. "Lashing. Stoning. Something barbaric."

Bushra looks at me. "I'm scared, Ghalib." Her voice is a whisper.

I've never known Bushra scared before. It frightens me. She's such a fighter. Such a strong spirit.

"We'll be out of Aleppo soon," I say.

Baba finds the west road at last and we leave the troubled Old City and head toward the town of Urum al-Kubra. The road opens out. As we walk farther from the city, I relax a little.

Cars and trucks sometimes pass us, but no minibuses or microbuses. We don't try to get a lift. "You don't know who might be driving," Baba says. We don't get offered any lifts either. "The driver doesn't know who he might be inviting into his vehicle."

People keep to themselves. It's safer that way.

We stop on a little tree-covered hill for a late lunch. Dayah, Dapir, and Bushra finally unpin their face veils and loosen their scarves. I gulp water as

Dayah and Dapir hand around pitas stuffed with cheese and canned tomatoes.

"How far is it, Baba?" I say.

"A long way on foot," he says. "I thought there would still be transport."

"Will we get there before dark?"

"I hope so."

"What if we don't?" Bushra says. She's been quiet up to now. She still looks scared.

"We're doing well, Bushra," Baba says. "We will reach town before dark. How are your feet, Ghalib?"

My feet have been stinging for the last hour, but I haven't said anything. And since we have so much farther to go before dark, I can't say anything now either. Dapir and Alan are doing so well. I don't want to be the one to hold everyone up.

"Not too bad," I say.

"I'll give you painkillers," Baba says. He opens his bag. "They'll help."

We don't linger after we've eaten. We pack up, take up our bags and walk again. We're not the only travelers along the route. Ahead and behind, people straggle along the length of the road. Sometimes we pass groups eating or resting. Sometimes families turn off the main road toward villages and farms.

The afternoon passes. We walk and walk. We no longer talk. There's too far to go and too much to carry.

The heat burns out of the day; the painkillers burn out of my system. My feet are on fire. Every step feels like I'm walking on knives.

We shift the bags around and Baba carries Alan for a while. The air turns golden.

Bushra peers at the evening sky. "It is far now, Baba?"

"Not far."

We're still some distance from Urum al-Kubra when I see blue smoke-haze hanging like cobwebs around the trees rambling up the hills. Bushra walks close to Dayah as we near the town. Alan climbs off Baba's back and slips his hand into mine.

"What's the smell?" he says.

"Burning," I say.

As we get nearer, the first of the red-roofed homes trail up the hillsides. There are no columns of smoke, no dark clouds staining the blue, but already we see blackened, broken buildings. The burning smell gets stronger as the road drops into the town. There are no Kurdish Protection Units in this part of Syria. Baba is watchful. His wariness frightens me. My skin tightens on my bones. We could be walking into anything.

"Who controls the town, Baba?" I say.

"Syrian army."

"Will they kill us?"

"We're no threat to them. We're just passing through."

The first of the town houses look empty: windows shuttered, doors locked, vegetable gardens overgrown and untended. There are no cars or vans on the streets.

"I hope we find somewhere to stay," Bushra says. I hope so too. It's been such a long walk.

We turn a corner. A tank blocks the width of the road. Three soldiers of the Syrian army lean against it. They swing their guns around, snap into action, but quickly relax when they focus on us. My heart pounds as we near them. I keep my eyes on the ground. Look back to see where Dayah is. She touches my shoulder. "Relax, Ghalib." Her voice is soft.

We squeeze past the tank. The smells of hot metal and of the soldiers' sweat catch in my throat. I thought when we left Kobani and Aleppo, we would see no more fighting. I thought it was behind us.

We pass by. I don't look back. We turn onto an empty street, with no soldiers or tanks or hot metal smell. Only old smoke and abandoned houses.

"Can we get water to drink in one of these houses?" Bushra says.

"Those are people's homes," Baba says. "We have no permission to enter."

"It's only water," Bushra says. But she mutters it under her breath so only I hear.

Near the town center we find a small shop. Dayah and Dapir buy bottles of water, oranges and pastries.

"The shopkeeper's wife has room in her house," Dayah says. "He says we can stay tonight."

"Alhamdulillah," Bushra says. "We will be safe."

The shopkeeper lives in a two-story house outside town, with weavings and wall hangings that remind me of home. In the separate kitchen at the back, his wife pours basins of hot water for us to wash. Baba cleans and dresses my feet. Some blisters have burst and stuck to the bandages. Tears run down my face.

"You're brave," Baba says.

Afterward, the shopkeeper's wife serves us home-grown vegetables, fried chicken and bread, and hot sweet tea. The food tastes wonderful.

"It's been so long since we've had fresh vegetables," Dapir says to our hosts. "And meat."

Bushra, Alan, and I roll out our bedrolls and blankets on the floor in the front room. Dayah and Baba sleep in a small recess off the kitchen, while Dapir has a proper bed upstairs.

"Our first night away from home, Bushra," I say.

"A good place," Bushra says. "A safe place."

It's certainly peaceful here, with no bombs or air-strikes. Even so, I can't sleep. I listen to the sounds, so different from home: snuffles and rustling of small animals, the odd cluck from the woman's hens.

The cockerel crows the next morning when it's still dark. The woman fills our water keg with fresh water, serves us hard-boiled eggs from her hens, and gives Dayah a loaf of her bread, wrapped in a clean cloth, for the road.

"The border is two days away," she says. "You might find somewhere to stay in Tal Al Karama, a village near the Roman road. You should reach there this evening. A quiet road through pine woods and bare hills."

Baba pays the shopkeeper, who loads his wheel-barrow with our bags and walks us to the road that leads to Tal Al Karama. He blesses our journey; we thank him and walk on.

7

"Carry me, Ghalib," Alan says.

"I can't carry you *and* the bags."

"I'm tired. My leg hurts."

We've been walking a long time. It's late afternoon. Apart from short rests and a break for lunch, we've hardly stopped since we left the shopkeeper's house in Urum al-Kubra. Now the bedroll Alan's been carrying on his back hangs off his shoulder. His face is flushed and his bad leg throws a spit of dust with every step. I put down my bags to fix him.

"Don't stop, Ghalib," Baba says. "We've a way to go yet."

"Two minutes," I say.

"Come on, Alan, you're a big boy," Baba says. "You can rest later."

I straighten the straps on Alan's bag, pull out his T-shirt from where it bunches at his shoulder. The cloth is damp. I give him a drink from my water bottle. He twines his arms around my shoulders and raises his leg, getting ready to climb into my arms.

"I can't carry you with the bags," I say again.

"Leave the bags," he says. "Just carry me."

I laugh. "The bags have our clothes and food. They're important."

"I'm more important."

I take his hot hand in mine. "We'll walk together."

Dayah and Dapir are in front of Baba and Bushra. Dapir walks slowly but doesn't stop. She hasn't stopped since we started. She carries her own bag and plods on. She walked everywhere in Kobani, even when Dayah had money for a shared taxi home from market. I look at her now as she leads us through this wild place. She doesn't complain about the heat or the distance or her tired legs.

"Let's show Dapir how good you are at walking," I say to Alan.

Half a dozen steps ahead of us, a stone hops straight up from the dusty road. It tumbles down and clatters against its neighbors. I stare at it. A distant crack echoes through the hills. I'm still figuring what happened when another rock farther away shatters in a shower of dust and splintered stone. It too is followed by a sharp blast. The unmistakable sound of gunshot.

"Sniper!" I shout.

I drop our bags. Fling myself onto the dirt road. Dragging Alan with me, I roll into the dry ditch. With a shock of terror, I squeeze my eyes shut and am instantly back in the bombed-out building in Kobani, sucking in hot burning air and hunting for Hamza. Panic surges through me.

Alan howls for Dayah. I snap open my eyes. I'm in a ditch beside the dirt road. Snipers are shooting at us.

"I'm here, Alan," I say. "Are you hurt?"

He shakes his head. Tears run down his dusty face. "I want Dayah," he says.

A hundred paces away, the rest of the family huddles in the dirt in a tight little knot, half hidden by rising dust. I wish we were next to them. They're a long way from where we're hiding. If I hadn't stopped to fix Alan, we would be beside them now.

Baba shouts at us. "Are you hurt?"

I call back to him. "We're fine!"

"Keep down. Stay low." He reaches for the bags to pull around them. I want to do the same, but can't move. I'm paralyzed with terror. Alan sobs. He's getting himself worked up to howl. I think fast.

"See if you can see the shooters," I say.

He snivels and squints into the distance, searching the stony brown hills. I try to work out who might be shooting. The shopkeeper's wife said there would be no trouble along this road. ISIS is nowhere around. Kurds live in these villages. Why would someone shoot at us? We don't look like rebels or armed forces. We carry only clothes and food.

The crack of a gun explodes through the hills again. Alan screams and clings to me. He trembles. This time there are no explosions of pulverized rock. No hopping stones. The shooters have hit nothing. Three times now they've missed. How could they miss six people on an open road?

"They're not trained shooters," I say.

"There, Ghalib!" Alan says.

He points to a cluster of ruins on the flank of the hill rising from the road. A couple of broken houses. Fields with collapsed stone walls. I watch until— there! A small figure peers briefly from behind a wall. Not a man. Not an adult. ISIS child soldiers are as skilled as adults, but I already know this sniper can't aim. It's not ISIS. It's not the Syrian army. It's just one small and ineffective sniper.

My courage rises. It pushes back my fear. It gives me strength.

On the other side of the road, halfway between where we're huddled and where Baba and the others are, is an abandoned house: stone walls, no roof, no doors. Tangled garden. I heft myself onto my haunches.

"Where are you going?" Alan says.

"We can't stay here."

"Stay there, Ghalib!" Baba says. "It's too dangerous."

But I've already decided the under-sized shooter can't hit anything. I grab Alan by the hand. He pulls back.

"Baba says it's dangerous," he says.

"Baba can't see what we see," I say. "Come on. We'll run together."

We leave our bags. We stay low and dash the short distance to the ruin. Alan limps and scampers. He has forgotten his exhaustion and his sore leg. We dive through the gaping doorway as the sniper fires off another couple of shots. The crack of the gun rings loud and frightening in the hills. Baba shouts in panic, but we're safe behind solid stone walls. And as I guessed, the bullets don't hit anything.

"We're fine," I say. "It's better in here."

We can stand up now. Move around, safe and protected. I dust off our clothes. Wipe tears from Alan's grimy face. "You were really brave," I tell him. "He can't shoot us in here."

"Will he kill us?"

"Not if I kill him first," I say.

My words sound braver than I feel. My heart pounds and my hands shake, but I won't let a sniper beat me. At the open window, we peek out at the rest of the family. Alan waves at Baba.

"You can make it," I say to Baba. "It's only one shooter. He misses every time."

But Baba won't leave the others, even when he sees the shooter peek from behind his hillside hide-out. Bushra makes the first move. She locks her eyes on the sniper. She waits for the right moment.

"Come on, Bushra!" I say.

And she's off. Without saying anything to Baba, Bushra pelts from the ditch and races toward us. Keeping a smooth stride, she even manages to snatch up a bag on her way. My blood sings to see her run. Fireworks explode in my belly when she bursts through the door of the little ruined house, eyes shining, face beaming.

"I made it!" she says.

Alan jumps up and down. We cheer with excitement. "The sniper didn't fire," I say.

"Maybe he's reloading."

We hunker down and wait. There is silence for a long time. Dapir, Baba and Dayah are still in the ditch.

"They'll still be there tomorrow," Bushra says.

"Come on!" Alan says. "It's easy!"

After a while, Dapir shifts.

"She's coming before her son!" Bushra says.

This is not good: Dapir isn't swift like my sister, though she has the same brave spirit.

But she doesn't try to run or even to move fast. She is Dapir. She walks with the grace and stiffness of an old lady, stepping deliberately and carefully across the stony road. I hold my breath the entire time; Alan buries his face in my side. Bushra crouches frozen next to me. There is no gunfire, no hopping stones. The sniper holds off. We run to the door to greet Dapir. To draw her into the shelter of our little ruined cottage. To hug and kiss her.

"That sniper knew there was no point shooting old bones like mine," Dapir says.

When I hold her hands, they tremble. In spite of her brave deed and fighting words, she was frightened.

In the end, Baba and Dayah are shamed out of the ditch. Dayah runs first, holding her dress and grabbing a bag as she saw Bushra do. The sniper shoots wide and wild as Dayah is almost at the door of the house. We scream.

I grab Dayah's hand and pull her to safety. Dayah yelps and ducks inside. As before, the bullets ring hollow and hit nothing, but we're not any less frightened. We're still hugging Dayah, to comfort and reassure her, when two more shots split the air. I spin around as Baba lunges through the doorway, the water keg and medical pouch in his arms.

"You made a run for it!" I say.

Giddy with relief, we cheer and laugh.

"It's not funny," Baba says. Sweat stains his shirt.

"Maybe a little funny," Bushra says. "That shooter can't hit anything."

"He's practicing hard," Dapir says. "He'll get it right yet."

"What if he comes here?" Alan says.

That sobers us up. Now that Alan has put it out there, I can't relax thinking the sniper might come after us. I peek out the gaping windows. Peer up the hillside where we saw the figure. Scan the empty land all around.

"Nobody there," I say.

"We're safe for now," Baba says. "We won't move from here."

We hunker down in a shady corner to wait it out, sitting quietly within the solid walls. We listen for anyone approaching but the only sounds in the barren countryside are a lark, high overhead, and the soft breeze whispering past the walls of the little house.

"How long do we wait?" I say. I keep my voice low.

"However long it takes," Baba says.

Which is not really an answer at all. I say nothing. The unexpected rest is welcome anyhow.

"Who's hungry?" Dayah says. She rummages in the bags, unwraps the fresh bread from the shopkeeper's wife, and breaks it apart. She lays out hardboiled eggs, cucumber, tomatoes. Dapir cuts wedges of sheep's cheese. There are no more gunshots.

"If there wasn't a shooter trying to blast us apart," Bushra says, "this would be a nice picnic."

"Maybe he's gone," Alan says.

After I've eaten, I peep out the rear windows again.

The hills are still wild and empty. I shimmy to the door and look out. Nothing moves. Fifty paces back, our bags are scattered on the road where we flung them.

"I'll get one of the bags," I say.

"You'll stay here!" Dayah says.

"It'll test if he's gone."

"And if he's not?" Dayah says.

"He can't hit anything anyway. He's tried hard enough."

"And he's probably out of ammo by now," Bushra says.

"We'll find out," I say.

"Ghalib," Dayah says. Her words ring with warning.

"We can't wait it out here forever, Dayah!"

Dayah looks at Baba. "Tell him not to go."

"None of the shots came near us, Gardina," Baba says.

Dayah says nothing, which I take as tacit approval, though it could also be that she's annoyed with Baba. Bushra nods her support to me.

I make my move. Slowly I emerge from the open doorway, checking up and down the empty road. I aim for the nearest bag. If any shots are fired, I'll dive into the ditch. I brace myself. One, two, three. I sprint down the road. I skid to a stop over loose stones. Snatch up the bag and fly back, bursting into the house less than a minute later.

I hold my trophy above my head. "Got it!"

There are no shots. No crack of gunfire. The hills remain wild and empty.

"He must be gone," Bushra says.

"I'll get another bag," I say. I peer out the gaping windows. Check the empty land.

And I'm off again.

I'm twenty paces along when I see the shooter in the middle of the road, rifling through our luggage. The gun is held aloft and ready to shoot.

I try to stop myself, but I'm at full pelt. I slither and slide over loose shale. I slew to a stop. It's too late to retreat. I've already been seen. My heart leaps to my throat when the shooter's head rises. I stare straight into the sniper's eyes.

8

The shooter is a girl. She looks about the same age as me. I stare at her, unable to tear my gaze from her face. Her eyes mesmerize me. They're dark, almost black. They hold more anger and sadness than I've ever seen. And something else too, something hidden deep that reminds me of the wild cat that reared her ginger kittens in the alley behind our house. She spat and hissed if you went closer than ten paces. This girl looks ready to spit and hiss too.

Her tangle of black matted hair is tied off her scrawny face with a bright beaded *keffiyeh*, but otherwise allowed to stick out however it likes. She is dressed in a striped cotton tunic. Long skirts. Beaded waistcoat. She crouches over my sports bag, one of her filthy hands on the zip, the other gripping her rifle. My eyes flicker to the gun, but that's not what freezes me to the spot. It's her stare. She has a dangerous and defiant stare. She looks me up and down as though I am in the wrong. As though trying to decide whether or not to shoot me. I want to turn and run, but I can't move.

"Why?" I say. It's all I can think of.

"Food." Her voice is dry, her lips cracked.

"There's none."

"Water."

She has lines around her eyes like Dapir. Tired lines. She's too young to have an old person's lines. And sores around her mouth.

"There's no water either," I say.

"Everyone has food and water."

She tugs open the zipper and yanks out my clothes, my games. Flings them to the road.

"Hey! Those are mine." Anger overrides my fear.

She jerks her head up. "Where is the food and water?"

"Inside." I point back toward the house.

Her dark eyes flicker and then flash back to me. "Get it."

"Come with me," I say, though as soon as the words are out of my mouth, I regret my dangerous challenge. My family is safe for now. If I bring this girl in, that could change.

She lifts her gun. "Get it or I'll kill you."

A girl of action, clearly not open to conversation. I decide she's bluffing. I don't think she ever intended to hit us earlier, only spook us. Maybe she's not a poor shot at all, just a reluctant sniper. And desperate for food and water.

"Wait here," I say.

Inside the house, Bushra and Alan spin around to see if I've managed to get another bag. I take bread and cheese from our leftover meal and a bottle of water. Baba watches me but says nothing.

"What are you doing?" Dayah says.

"Back in a minute," I say.

Outside, the girl has discarded my bag. The zipper is open, but she's stuffed my belongings back. She waits, gun beside her. When I step close to hand over the food, she stiffens and swings up the weapon. I stop short, place the food on my bag and step back. She pounces. Stuffs bread and cheese into her mouth, gulps down water. She packs some food inside her tunic.

"Medicine?" she says.

She doesn't look in need of medicine. But maybe other snipers are in the hills. Others who need medicine and the food she's hidden.

"What medicine?" I say.

She reaches for her gun. "Get it or I'll kill you." Here we go again.

"I need to know what medicine," I say.

"I don't know."

I sigh. "Wait."

I return to the house and, again, everyone turns to see. "The shooter is outside," I say. "A girl. She needs medicine."

"Is she threatening you?" Baba says.

"I don't think she's going to kill us. But she has a gun."

"Well, that's one way to get help." He gets his medical pouch.

"Can I come?" Alan says.

"You stay right here," says Dayah. She pulls Alan into her lap, looks at me and Baba. "Be careful."

When she sees my father, the girl retreats and lifts her gun. "Who's this?"

"The man with the medicine," I say.

"I don't want him." Her voice is raised now, dark eyes flashing anger. Her gaze jumps from my face to Baba's.

"I have medicine," Baba says. "I can help. Put down your gun."

The girl hesitates. She still holds her gun but doesn't point it. Her eyes don't flash the same anger. She jerks her head toward me.

"He comes too," she says. Baba looks at me. I nod.

She leads us up ancient goat trails and sheep paths, through scrubby grass and meadows of mountain flowers, toward the cluster of small ruins Alan spotted earlier. She leaps with ease across small ravines and cuts in the hills. Baba and I are slower. Several times she waits for us to catch up.

We're out of breath by the time we reach the settlement. There are a couple of outhouses, a little courtyard, fields, an outhouse off to one side. Most of it is in ruins. Tufts of grass and weeds poke through broken slabs. Nobody has lived here for a long time.

"Wait here," the girl says.

She disappears into one of the buildings. When she returns, the gun and the food she stuffed inside her clothes are both gone.

"Come on," she says to Baba. And to me, "Wait."

Baba follows her into the house. A rash of fear prickles the back of my neck. I hold my breath. Listen for gunshots or raised voices but only the soft sigh of wind whispers through the grasses and bobs the heads of tiny flowers. I gaze down the hillside to where the others are sheltering in the little stone house. Sweat itches my back.

Baba and the girl are gone a long time. The sun is dropping in the sky by the time they come out. The girl carries an armful of clothing, her gun, an old bag stuffed with belongings. An ammunition belt with bullets is slung around her body. She glances at me and again I see something a little wild, a little frightening in her dark eyes. Baba follows, carrying a small bundle wrapped in filthy blankets. I can't see who is inside.

"Get my bag, Ghalib," Baba says. He jerks his head toward the doorway behind him. "Then lead me down the hill."

Inside the little house my eyes take a moment to adjust to the dim light. I search the dark corners, but the place is empty. No furniture either. They were sleeping on the earth floor. From the smell of the place, they haven't been using the privy. A bundle of soiled blankets is bunched in the corner, the remains of the food scattered next to it. I snatch up Baba's pouch and run out, eager to get back to the clean air.

The descent is slower than our climb. Baba moves slowly down the hillside with his bundle. I stay close to warn him of gaps between the rocks where he could fall. The girl hops and leaps ahead of us. She's familiar with the layout of the land, but anxious about the person in Baba's arms. She repeatedly circles back to check under the blanket, touching the feet, the hands. Her concern is unexpected, in stark contrast with her hostility toward us. She ignores me entirely, in spite of wanting me to come in the first place. Eventually we step onto the road. The air blues with evening as we enter the little ruin.

Dayah jumps up to help when she sees Baba with a patient. "What happened?"

The girl hangs back at the open doorway watching us with dark eyes, taking in everything. Her movements are restless and agitated.

"High fever," Baba says. "Dehydration. Not taking anything by mouth. We need to bring his temperature down. Set up an IV."

He pulls the blankets open. A small boy—younger than Alan—lies in soiled clothes, his eyes sunken and closed, long lashes flickering. His pale limbs are thin, the skin dry. Dayah pulls off his filthy clothing and stained blankets, washes him with a damp cloth. I fill a water bottle from the large keg and mix in rehydration salts. Baba sets it up with a syringe to get fluids into the boy. He lays him on one of our bedrolls. In spite of his weakness, the boy refuses to let go of a grubby headscarf gripped in one hand, pulling it to his crusted lips like a comfort blanket.

"Bring the bags in, Bushra," Dayah says. "We're staying overnight."

"*Here?*" Bushra says. "This isn't even a *place*. It's a ruin. There's no roof or door. Have you noticed?"

"Ghalib will help," Dayah says.

Bushra and I gather the bags, no longer in fear of being shot.

"Why are we helping a *sniper?*" Bushra says. "She still has her gun with her."

"A good reason to help her," I say. "Just don't make her angry."

We stack the bags against the wall.

"I'm not sleeping near someone who tried to kill us," Bushra says.

"That's enough, Bushra," Baba says.

There's no more discussion, but Bushra makes her feelings clear. She sighs. Throws her eyes up to the sky. Turns her back on the girl.

The temperature drops with the sun. We light a little fire with wood we find behind the house, heat water for sweet tea and sit under the stars. The girl remains at the threshold, crouched among her bags and blankets, gun propped across her lap. She accepts a cup of sweet tea when I bring it to her but says nothing. Soon after it gets dark, we lay out our quilts and blankets around the blaze and settle down for the night. Baba stays close to his patient, adjusting the drip, checking his temperature. Bushra stays as far as possible from the girl, taking herself to the other side of the house.

I lie awake for a long time, listening to insects and little creeping creatures. To the snap and crackle of the fire. To the breathing of Dapir and Dayah. Before I finally fall asleep, I turn to where Bushra lies.

"Second night away from home, Bushra." My voice is soft, only a whisper. But she hears.

"Not a good place, Ghalib," she says.

\- - -

I wake to brilliant sunlight shining through the open roof. The ground beneath me is hard and rocky. My back is sore but the morning is clear and bright, and already the fire is lit to heat water. Dapir, Bushra, and Alan are still asleep, bundled together under blankets. Dayah prepares what food we have left for breakfast. Baba leans over the boy, checking how he is. The girl is curled next to him, sharing his quilt.

She must have sneaked in sometime during the night. She's asleep.

I creep to Baba's side. "How is he?"

"Doing well. On his third infusion with antibiotics."

The girl stirs. Her dark eyes fly open. She leaps from the ground onto her haunches, instantly alert. Her fingers tighten around her gun. She flashes her gaze to the boy, reaching to touch his face with her grubby fingertips. Her sudden softness is startling. The boy doesn't stir. The girl looks at my father.

"He's fine," Baba says. "He's sleeping and his temperature has come down."

The girl checks where everyone is, as though confirming her safety. Her shoulders drop a little. Her wariness eases.

"What's his name?" Baba says.

She looks at him with her startling black eyes. She glances at me. "Amin," says the girl.

"Your brother?"

She nods.

"And your name?"

She says nothing at first, chewing her lip before she answers. "Safaa," she says eventually.

"Where are your parents, Safaa?" Baba says.

"Killed." Her voice is little more than a whisper.

"In the war?"

She nods.

"We'll wake Amin in a little while and see if we can get him to eat," Baba says.

Dayah brings us each a cup of sweet tea. "Sip it slowly," she says. "It's the last of the water."

By the time the air warms, everyone is up and moving around. Alan is stiff in the morning. It takes him a little while to get his bad leg going. He hops around awkwardly, peering curiously at Amin and Safaa. For her part, Safaa spends a fair amount of time staring at him, or more particularly at his bad leg, but with none of the hostility she reserves for the rest of us. Bushra and Safaa ignore each other completely.

We spread out our bedding to dry in the morning sun, then eat the last of the bread and cheese.

"We need to get more food in the next village," Dayah says.

"What's left?" I say.

"Eggs. A few tomatoes."

"That's it?" says Bushra. "We have to walk through a desert with no water?"

"Tal Al Karama is an hour away," says Safaa.

We stare at her in surprise. It's the first thing she has volunteered.

It turns out we don't need to wake Amin. Maybe the medicines have taken effect, or our voices penetrate his slumber, or the warm sunlight rouses him, but he sits up unexpectedly and looks around, matted hair clumped and sticking out in all directions, much like his sister's.

"Safaa?" he says in a broken little voice.

She is beside him in an instant, muttering soothing words. Stroking his face and hands. Baba examines him, encourages him to eat small pieces of bread, to sip a little cooled sweet tea. Considering how sick he was, Amin comes around quickly. He's scrawny and pale, but his shriveled look has faded. Dayah gives Safaa some of Alan's clean clothes to dress her brother. Safaa rolls up the legs of the tracksuit, tucks in the clean T-shirt. Amin manages a few wobbly steps, clinging to Safaa's arm. Alan is fascinated by him and hovers close by.

"You can't stay up in those hills," Baba says to Safaa. "He's not well enough yet. He needs proper care, and you both need food."

He looks at her and Amin. A look passes between him and Dayah that means more than we're supposed to know. Alan is too young and doesn't notice, while Bushra doesn't want anything to do with Safaa. But I notice. And I understand.

"Will you and Amin come with us?" Baba says. "You're welcome to travel with my family as far as the village. Farther if you wish."

"Baba!" Bushra says. I hear the hiss in her words. "We *can't*!"

But even as Bushra speaks, dark anger surges into Safaa's face. It flashes in her eyes. She stares at Baba with that defiant look that mesmerized me the first time I saw her. "I don't need your help."

"I think you do," Baba says. His voice is quiet.

"You can't stay here, Safaa," Dayah says. Her words are persuasive, her voice soft. "You won't get proper food or medicine by shooting travelers on the road. What happens if Amin gets sick again? Or if you get hurt?"

Anger gleams from Safaa's dark eyes, but she listens to Dayah's words. She hears the truth. One part of my heart understands her conflict, her uncertainty.

"Come as far as Tal Al Karama," Dayah says. "You can leave us then if you choose."

Ultimately it's Amin who changes Safaa's mind. He slips his small hand into hers, tugging for attention.

"Not back up the hill, Safaa," he says in his funny cracked little voice. "Please."

Safaa picks Amin up. She murmurs to him. She turns to us as he clings to her. "We'll come with you."

But Baba is clear about one thing.

"We won't travel with your gun," he says. "Leave it here."

Safaa looks uncertain. For a moment I think she might change her mind and retreat into the barren hills with her brother. If she does, Amin will not survive, and Safaa might not either. Maybe the same thought runs through her head. She's angry and defiant and dangerous, but she is smart. She looks at me briefly. As though reading my thoughts, she makes her decision. She crams her gun in a crack in the wall of the ruined house, with her belt of bullets. She packs small stones and rocks over the hiding place.

"My gun will be here for me," she says. "Or for someone else."

Amin can't walk far yet, so we rearrange our luggage. Baba carries him. In return, Safaa carries the water keg—which is now empty—and her own bundle. The rest of the bags are shared among us. Eight of us walk out of the ruined house toward Tal Al Karama.

9

The road is longer and harder for all of us on our third day walking. The luggage feels heavier, which makes no sense: we've eaten most of the food, so our bags should be lighter. My muscles are stiff and my feet ache. I didn't expect to walk so far and so long. All over Syria, people use microbuses, minibuses, and shared taxis to get around, and buses for far-off cities. Since we left the minibus on the outskirts of Aleppo, I've only seen a few shared taxis. It seems this war has cleared the roads of almost everything else.

So much walking is especially hard for Alan. "My leg is tired," he says after we've been on the road for no more than half an hour.

"It's too early to be tired, Alan," Baba says.

Dayah massages Alan's weak leg like she used to do when he was a toddler struggling to balance and walk for the first time. A physical therapist showed her exercises and stretches to help him. Safaa and Amin stare at Alan now but say nothing.

Dapir finds the walking hard too, but for different reasons. Back home, it always takes a while for her morning stiffness to wear off. In Kobani, she sat on the sofa, watching the street, for an hour or two in the morning, sipping her sweet tea, before beginning her chores. But that's not possible here.

"I'll take your bag, Dapir," Bushra says.

Dapir is proud and independent—she never wants anyone to do things for her. But now she hands her bag over to Bushra. She presses her free hand against her hip as though supporting it. In turn, I take one of Bushra's bags.

"How are your feet?" Baba says to me.

"They'll be better when we arrive this evening," I say.

"I'll dress them tonight. And when we get to Tal Al Karama and get water, I'll give you the same painkillers you had yesterday."

Unlike the rest of us, Safaa strides to Tal Al Karama. She doesn't speak to us, and not much more to Amin, but focuses on the road ahead. Strong.

Bold. I can't stop looking at her, half afraid of her, half fascinated by her. She wears her sniper spirit brazenly. In stark contrast, she also carries the deep concern and gentleness I first saw yesterday in her anxiety for her little brother. Today, she stays close to Baba to hold Amin's hand. She murmurs to him occasionally in an unfamiliar language. Amin is still and quiet as long as she's close, but frets if she's out of his sight. Her presence keeps him calm.

The road to Tal Al Karama is not entirely empty. Military trucks speed by occasionally, raising clouds of dust and spits of gravel. Rows of uniformed soldiers stare out at us, gun muzzles pointing upward from between their knees. Sometimes a jeep rolls by, and once we see a tank, which causes great excitement for Alan and Amin but a spike of fear for the rest of us. Pine trees trail over the hills around us and line the roadside. Burnt-out cars rust in the ditch. Empty houses crumble into the dirt.

"No shortage of accommodation," Bushra says as we pass yet another abandoned ruin.

Tal Al Karama is a village of stone houses and battle-damaged streets. We crunch over shattered glass and bricks. Pass two churches and a mosque, all of which show scars of bullets and explosions.

Laundry hangs to dry on the flat rooftops of several houses. A child peers down from a broken window.

Safaa is familiar with the layout of the village. Silently, she leads us through narrow streets, turning left and right. Two women pass, carrying containers for water or fuel. They look at us but say nothing. Some of the houses have their doors open to the air and I glimpse hens, a cat, a couple of men, in the inner courtyards. We arrive at a small square with a few market stalls busy with local shoppers filling their baskets. We lower our bags to the steps of a large municipal building and sink to the cool stone to rest and take stock. Baba puts Amin down gently and checks how he is—peering into his eyes, taking his pulse. Amin's head wobbles but he smiles at Baba.

Safaa points to the far side of the square, where a carved lion's head trickles water into a moss-green stone trough. While Dayah and Bushra buy food at the stalls, Alan goes with Baba to fill the water keg. Safaa walks Amin a little way into the market while I sit with Dapir and the luggage. Within half an hour, we're fed and hydrated and have enough food to keep us going for the day. Baba gives me painkillers, and encourages Amin to drink a little more. As we gather up our bags to move on, Safaa looks uncertain, in contrast to her earlier demeanor.

"Will you stay here, or come with us?" Baba says.

Safaa looks at each of us in turn, stroking Amin's hand as she does so. Her eyes linger on Alan, and then on me, which sends a shiver up my spine. One part of me wants her to leave my family. To stay here in the village with her brother. That's the safer thing to do. But a bigger part of me is a little excited she might come with us. She's interesting and a bit scary.

"We'll come," she says.

A little thrill sparks in my belly as we walk out of Tal Al Karama and take the road for the border.

"How far, Baba?" I say.

"We should be there by early afternoon. We'll take the quiet road and meet up with main traffic routes closer to the border."

The quiet road leads through mostly undamaged farmland. Goats graze around scrubby bushes. Local farmers tend to their olive trees in stony fields. Travelers like us tramp along, weighed down with bags and babies. The countryside is scattered with Roman remains from centuries past—blocks of carved stone and broken columns and foundations—overgrown with vines and brambles. We pass a cemetery where

I stare at dozens of fresh graves, most without even grave markers on them. On a steep slope, a paved road runs parallel to our route, bordered with pines and a stone wall. Limestone slabs rimmed by thick moss and grasses glare whitely in the sun.

"Must be the Roman road the shopkeeper's wife mentioned," Baba says.

As the day passes, I notice Alan too is drawn to Safaa, even though he can't keep up with her determined pace. Whenever we take a break, he sits close to her, watching her interactions with Amin. And for her part, she tolerates him better than she does any of the rest of us, even breaking off some of her bread to give him at lunchtime. Bushra sees me looking.

"Keep Alan away from that sniper," she says.

"I don't think she'll hurt him."

"She'll poison his mind with her talk of guns and shooting."

I turn to Baba. "What language does she even speak?"

"Sounds like Armenian," Baba says.

Shortly after lunch, we arrive at a junction where four roads meet. "The main road to Bab al-Hawa," Baba says. The Turkish border.

We buy sweet tea at a makeshift café and cool it with our breath, standing with a dozen other travelers. The road is busy with vehicles and walkers, all heading in the same direction.

The line of traffic begins long before Bab al-Hawa is even in sight. Trucks, vans, and buses line the dusty highway winding through the brown hills. Nothing moves. Engines idle, filling the air with fumes. Other vehicles sit silent, doors and windows open for air. Whole families are squashed inside the few shared taxis in the line, bags and bundles packed around them. They stare out at us as we pass. Truck drivers circle their vehicles, getting onto their hands and knees to check around the axles. One climbs up to inspect the roof.

"What are they looking for?" I say.

"Checking that nobody has sneaked on to cross the border," Baba says.

"What would happen if they did?"

"The trucks would be turned back from the border and fined. Maybe even banned from crossing."

I look at the drivers. Sweating, greasy, they frown at anyone who lingers near. "Would they take us across if we paid them?"

"We would have to pay a lot," Baba says. "More than we have."

"But would they? If we did pay enough?"

"Maybe," Baba says. "It's a big risk for them. They might lose their jobs, maybe their families, if they got stuck on the wrong side of the border. Or their lives if they ended up back in Syria."

"What would happen if we hid on a truck?"

"Border guards have guns, Ghalib. Their job is to secure the border to Turkey. They're not going to care what happens to people hiding illegally."

The hot metal of the trucks, the reek of diesel fumes, the smoke from the drivers' cigarettes, all mingle in the thick air. A headache throbs behind my eyes. My burned feet sting me. I want to rest, but Baba is determined to reach the border before we stop.

"We'll have time to rest later," he says.

Dapir has slowed down. The endless walking has finally tired her out. She doesn't complain—Dapir never complains—but she trails at the back with Dayah, holding Alan's good hand. Her slower pace suits Alan. His gimpy leg slows him as it swings and kicks, swings and kicks. Bushra walks in front of them. She's not saying much today, which is new for Bushra. She carries Dapir's bags.

In contrast to Dapir, Amin seems stronger than before. He eats everything he's given and Baba makes sure he drinks lots of water. He walks for a little while alongside his sister, his comfort scarf clumped in his fist, then climbs into Safaa's arms like a little monkey. She scoops him up without a word. They hardly speak, even to each other. They have a way of communicating that doesn't need words: a look, a gesture, a poke—mostly from Safaa to Amin. She's figured out a way to carry their belongings and her brother without breaking the rhythm of her walk: she ties her roll onto her back in a complicated way with a long woven scarf so that she can carry it and him at the same time.

I walk in front with Baba. We will lead the others across the border into a new country. Into a new life.

A cluster of low buildings straddles the highway. It halts the stream of people who spill off the road to fill the stony land on either side like a stain stretching across the brown earth. The countryside beyond the low buildings is mostly empty: a few figures and a handful of vehicles move along a bare highway.

"Will we cross tonight?" I say.

"I don't know when we'll cross," Baba says.

I imagined we would cross before sunset, reach whatever town lies beyond the hills, and find a guesthouse. I imagined we would begin our new lives tomorrow.

"Why stay in Syria when we've come this far?"

Baba's face is grim. "We don't have the right papers. The government stopped issuing passports months back."

"Because of the war?"

He nods. "Another way to control people."

Fear slices through me. "Why come to the border if we don't have papers?"

"You know why we came," Baba says. "I don't need to tell you."

"But we might not get out."

"We have to try," Baba says. "If it takes a lifetime to cross, if we get separated, if we're unsuccessful, we still have to try."

I stare at the crowded border with its milling people. Its endless lines of vehicles. Its armed border guards. I think of Baba's words: things I've never considered. Frightening things. I look back at Alan and Dapir. At Safaa and Amin. They don't question where we're going. They don't ask why. They just follow us to the border.

"Could it take a lifetime to cross?" I say. "Could we get separated or be unsuccessful?"

"We'll think positively," Baba says. "We've made it this far. We're together. Let's keep those things in our heads and in our hearts."

A smile breaks across his face, but it looks like he had to dig deep to pull it up.

10

A large two-story building dominates the border, with a flat-roofed canopy straddling the highway. It looks new—its concrete bright, its paint fresh.

Turkish and Syrian flags flutter on its roof. Stretching as far as I can see are double rows of shiny barbed wire fixed to tall metal posts. The height of three men, they keep the countries separate. They keep Syrians out of Turkey.

We arrive among the heaving crowds who can't go farther. Men and women push forward. Babies and children cry and howl. The sweeping crowd grows thicker and stronger. It seethes and surges. It murmurs and shuffles. We no longer walk the highway among a stream of people. Instead we're swallowed up by a heaving throng. The energy in the midst of this chaos feels different. Threatening somehow.

"Stay together," Baba says.

He says something else about watching each other, but his words are swallowed up in the calls of a hundred people merging to become the voice of any father, any mother. We can no longer talk and be certain we'll be heard. Dayah and Dapir link arms. Alan lets go of Dapir and wriggles through the masses to my side. He clings to my leg. I grab him and check that Safaa and Amin are close by with Bushra.

Baba gestures with his arm and moves off the highway. We follow, pushing and weaving through distracted people, stepping over spiky shrubs clinging to the dusty earth. The frantic swell and shouts are behind us. The crowds are looser here. People move more slowly. Some even stand still, staring like they don't know where to go or what to do.

We pick our way to a place where people sit in groups among scrubby bushes. Men squat in circles, smoking. Women and children and old people sit or lie on the gravel. We follow Baba past crying babies and toddlers, past mothers with bundles and bags. Children snooze on spread-out blankets. Old people rummage in plastic bags. Packages and bags and tied rolls and bundles are heaped everywhere. An old woman sleeps in a wheelchair. Some groups have fashioned shelters with rugs and sheets of plastic draped over sticks poked in the ground. The ground is littered with torn food packages, babies' diapers, empty water bottles and spent cigarettes, dirty tissues, plastic bags. The stink of human waste and rotten food and other smells mingle together. Flies buzz in the air, drawn by dirt and debris. It's like a bombsite in Kobani.

We come to a space between two families.

"Here," Baba says. He swings his bag off his back. Sweat stains his shirt.

I look at the little patch of ground in the middle of so many families. To one side of us, two women stare into space. They lean against their bags, shoes kicked off, three small children lying beneath blankets next to them. On our other side, a young woman with a baby tied to her sits against her bedroll, gazing at us. Next to her, an old man lies on a blanket. Her father or father-in-law, I think. When I smile, she nods and shifts her dreaming elsewhere.

"Are we sleeping outside again?" Bushra's lip curls as she looks around. "This is worse than last night."

I wonder how long we'll stay here. We untie bedrolls, blankets, bags and bundles. Dayah spreads a blanket for Dapir, Alan, and Amin. The two small boys curl up immediately and will be asleep soon. Dayah sweeps Alan's hair from his hot face; Safaa spreads the loose end of Amin's grubby headscarf across him for shade. Dapir sits quietly. Her face is pale and drawn. She stares at nothing in particular. Bushra and Safaa hand out apples and crumbled cheese.

"Keep everything close," Baba says. "Especially water and food."

"How long will we be here?" Bushra says.

"Until we cross over," Baba says. "Ghalib, let's see what's happening."

"He's walked far enough today," Dayah says. "His feet."

My feet hurt, but I want to see more. "I'm fine, Dayah. I'll go with Baba."

Safaa stands up. "I'll come too."

I'm surprised, but Baba nods. Safaa checks that Amin is asleep, then follows us back to the highway. As the crowds thicken, I grasp Baba's shirt so I don't lose him. Behind me, I feel a light tug as Safaa holds my shirt. Something about her touch brightens the shadows dusking my blood. A smile pushes onto my face.

A deep trench has been gouged into the soil immediately in front of the double rows of barbed wire. A dry moat, several yards wide and equally deep. The bull-dozed earth is heaped in ridges and slopes beyond the trench. On these artificial hills, people hunker down to watch what's happening. Baba and I squat with them. Safaa stands next to us, a light breeze blowing her wild hair from her face. I watch her for a moment, then turn to the border.

Thick black and yellow columns support the concrete canopy of the Bab al-Hawa Crossing. Trucks line up but don't move forward. Half a dozen border guards with guns and walkie-talkies move between the buildings and the canopy, between waiting vehicles and people standing around. They talk on their walkie-talkies. They shout. They gesture and point. There are Syrian guards too, but not so many. Who wants to come to Syria anyway?

"Is it always as crazy as this?" Baba says to a man beside us.

"Anti-Turkish rebels set off a car bomb in Ankara, so the Turkish government shut the border," the man says. He spits on the ground. "They open it for a couple of hours a day for commercial trucks." He looks at the crowds walking the highway, the endless line of vehicles. "Everyone arrives in the afternoon. Nobody gets through."

"How long have you been here?" Baba says.

"A week." He wipes his beard. "Others are here a lot longer."

A week? How can anyone stay in this place for a week? No shelter. No kitchens. No shops or market. Just dry, empty land stretching as far as the horizon. A handful of scrubby trees. And endless barbed wire.

We squat in silence, watching the activity.

Safaa drops to her haunches next to us. "What happens if you get across?" she says. Her voice is soft.

The man points to a line of small vans in a lay-by on the Turkish side. "They'll take you into Reyhanli. If you pay them."

"Reyhanli?" I say.

"Nearest Turkish town. Half an hour away, I'm told."

The heat leaks from the sun. The light softens and turns the brown land golden. A quiet shifting ripples through the crowd. People drift off the slopes to return to their families. The surging crowd relaxes its energy. There are still long lines of buses and trucks, but drivers seem to have resigned themselves to spending the night in their vehicles. Engines are turned off. Doors and windows are closed against the coolness of night. As the sun drops behind the distant mountains, the light in the east takes on a blue haze. Shadows lengthen.

"Time to go back," Baba says.

We pick our way through family groups, past piles of bags and bundles. My feet burn when I start walking again on the stones and dirt off the highway. Every time I see a bright green scarf, I think it's Dayah. Every time I spot a striped bag on the ground, I think it's ours. Every time, I'm wrong.

"They were closer to the fence," I say.

"Not this close," Baba says. "I would remember the trench. They're over this way."

We never thought to note a landmark that would be easy to find.

"I have no idea where they are," Baba says.

Safaa looks at Baba and me with a withering expression. I've seen the same expression many times on Bushra's face. Safaa points to the border fence. High above the crowds, above the barbed wire, above the trench, a single Turkish flag flutters in the breeze.

"Follow it," she says.

And with a faint smile, she leads us through tired people and rubbish and empty water bottles, straight to where our family waits. *Smart Safaa*, I think.

"Where is Bushra?" Baba says.

"Gone to the sup-sup van," Dayah says.

"The *what?*"

Dayah points through the darkening distance to a white van that's pulled off the road, hazard lights flashing. Crowds mill around it. "Apparently it comes every evening with food and essentials," Dayah says. "Bushra has gone to get water and find out what they have."

"On her own?" Baba says.

"She'll be fine," Dayah says.

Having seen Safaa lead us safely back here, I don't have any concern for Bushra. But Baba can't settle. The light has seeped from the sky by the time my sister gets back with bottles of water and chocolate bars. She hands over a little change.

Dayah looks at the few coins. "Is that all?"

"He's charging crazy prices," Bushra says. She's furious. "Ripping people off."

"What is he selling?" Baba says.

"Diapers, potato chips, pastries. Biscuits and crackers," Bushra says.

Darkness falls. Families light cooking fires across the open air settlement. Soft firelight lifts the dense blackness. The smells of food cooking and cigarette smoke mask the reek of waste. At the border, flood-lights blaze into the night, shining on the canopy, the buildings, the endless barbed wire. Safaa and Dayah settle with the boys on the rug. Dapir and Bushra curl up, warm beneath blankets, and quickly start snoring. Baba and I look across the masses sleeping in the open air.

"Put a blanket around your shoulders," Baba says.

"I won't sleep," I say.

"You'll get cold. There's no heat in the air."

I pull a blanket over my shoulders and stare through the darkness. It's a clear night. A couple of trucks and buses move through the border checkpoint. Motors grind. Voices call out. A child cries somewhere. Strangers make noise in sleep or waking, every one of them dreaming of somewhere other than this stony patch of ground among strangers. They cough and whisper and snore, call out and turn and sigh.

I gaze at the stars from the Syrian horizon on one side to the Turkish horizon on the other. I think of the new life we'll have—a life of peace and happiness on the far side of the barbed wire fence, away from everything that is happening in Syria.

11

In spite of what I expect, I fall asleep sometime during the night. I wake shivering and pull my dew-damp blanket closer around my shoulders. My neck aches from lying crooked across the bags. Around me, people cough and spit in the blue dawn. Some pray, pressing foreheads and knees to the stony earth. Others walk around to stretch and wake up. Mothers comfort cold and crying children. A few sad fires smoke damply.

Dayah and Baba are both awake. Sitting side by side beneath the same rug, they talk quietly and look around the settlement with sleep-swollen eyes. Dapir, Alan and Bushra sleep on, barely visible beneath their shared blanket.

"Where are Amin and Safaa?" My voice cracks open the stillness of the morning like a broken egg.

I gaze around, searching pale tired faces nearby. I don't see Amin's worried little face, nor Safaa's wild hair anywhere. Safaa's main bundle is missing, but her small carpetbag lies on the ground.

"Baba?" I say.

"They weren't here when I woke up," Baba says.

"How long have they been gone?"

"I don't know," he says. "I don't know *where* they've gone either."

"It's early yet, Ghalib," my mother says. "They won't have gone far."

But her words don't bring any comfort. Why would they leave us? They stayed close and constant since Safaa first shot at us. They have no one else. Nowhere to go. Safaa doesn't even have her gun.

"They might be back in a little while," I say.

"Maybe they're at the sup-sup van," I say.

"Or maybe they needed to relieve themselves," I say.

"Stop going on about them," Bushra says. She pulls herself upright and looks around. "Good riddance to the sniper, I say."

While Bushra and Dapir stretch and rub their eyes, Baba and I bring Alan to the trench in front of the border fence where men and boys relieve themselves.

"We're peeing outside again," Alan says. He laughs in the rising sun.

It's harder for women to find privacy. Dapir, Dayah, and Bushra take one of the rugs and are gone for a long time. When they return, each has her own grumbles.

"Some men don't know how to behave or where to look when women are in the open," Dayah says.

"This place isn't dignified or proper for women," Dapir says.

"Dapir and Dayah didn't hold the blanket properly," Bushra says.

"I'm hungry," Alan says.

Dayah pulls open the bags. With Amin and Safaa missing, we have more food to share, although I would prefer they were with us and we had less to eat. I miss them.

We finish the water, share the last apple. Dayah hands around tiny pieces of chocolate. She gives more to Dapir and Alan—the oldest and the youngest. Safaa and Amin haven't returned by the time we're ready to walk to the border.

"Bring everything," Baba says. "We don't know if we'll be back"

"What about Safaa and Amin?" I say. "How will they find us?"

Baba looks sad. Maybe he's worried about them too. "Our family comes first, Ghalib. Safaa and Amin can find us near the border. We can't wait for them when we don't know where they are or when they'll be back."

"What about their bag?" I say.

Baba takes up his own luggage, ties the blankets over the empty water barrel, checks that nothing is left. He looks at me. I see something in his eyes.

"Bring it if you want, Ghalib," he says. "But we can't be responsible for their belongings when we don't know where they've gone."

Baba is right, but his words make me miserable. I take up my bags and bundles. I add Safaa's carpetbag, take Alan's hand and follow the others through the sleepers and the daydreamers and the half-awake. I peer down the highway where the rising sun flashes on the windows of the endless line of trucks and buses and cars. It looks as long as it was yesterday.

The crowds on the highway and sloping hills are not so frenzied yet. We move easily past shuffling people. Many families are still asleep but others must have left or been allowed across the border.

"Maybe we'll get across today," I say.

Bushra looks at me with Bushra-scorn in her eyes. We find a viewing spot on the fake hillside to watch the border. There aren't so many families and women crouching on the slopes. Not so many mothers and grandmothers and sisters. For the most part, women, children and old people wait off the highway for their men to come back and tell them what to do and where to go. But Kurdish women stay next to their men. They don't wait to be told what to do and where to go. They work with their husbands and sons, whether fighting in the army or sitting quietly on stony slopes to watch the border. In our family, Dapir and Dayah and Bushra watch with Alan and Baba and me as the border guards walk around with their guns and walkie-talkies, gesturing and pointing, pulling vehicles aside. All morning we sit. There's not much talking. Dapir and Alan doze. My own eyes get heavy as the heat of the sun warms my back. I think of Safaa and Amin. Where have they gone? What if little Amin gets sick again? Safaa had started to talk a little more—might have been beginning to trust us. And now she's gone.

"What have you learned, Ghalib?" Baba says.

He startles me from my daydreams. I look at him blankly.

"There's no point being at the border unless we learn something. Something to help us cross."

Before I can speak, Bushra says, "Six Turkish guards patrol the border. If one goes into the building, another comes out to cover him."

I stare at her

"And they never allow more than two vehicles under the canopy at one time," she says.

How did she learn so much so fast? I look at the Syrian guards, who have little to do in comparison to the Turks. Hardly any traffic comes from Turkey into Syria: just the occasional truck bringing supplies or making deliveries.

"Syrian guards aren't interested in who comes to the border from the Turkish side," I say. It's not much.

"Border guards send drivers into the building while they search the truck," Bushra says. "Then they search the underside and the roof."

I'm irritated with her now. She sees me look at her and a smirk shades her face for an instant.

"They don't search the inside of the truck until the driver comes back out," Bushra says.

I lock my eyes on the border to track activity. No longer am I watching random movements of guards. Now, I search for patterns, routines, behaviors.

"The guards always have their backs to the fence nearest the highway," I say. "They all carry guns. The only route for people on foot is beneath the canopy."

"Both of you have learned a lot," Baba says.

As the day wears on, crowds thicken on the hills. People come from the settlement; new arrivals move slowly along the highway, weighed down with bags and bundles. The man Baba and I spoke with on the first evening was right: afternoons are the busiest. I'm distracted by hunger and thirst: it's been a long time since we ate the apple and chocolate. We all want food.

"I have nothing," Dayah says.

"We'll go to the sup-sup van later," Baba says.

As the light shifts and the afternoon slides toward evening, a change ripples through the crowd. It seems every person on the slopes takes a deep breath and sits up. I turn to see. A family steps from the hordes to speak to the border guards. The man is in front of his wife and children. Three armed guards watch him. This is new: nobody has dared to approach the guards. The crowd is silent. Everyone stares. Everyone waits. Everyone watches the scene unfold.

"He should be careful," Baba says. "This is not good."

The man indicates his family. He points toward Turkey. He holds out his papers. The guards gesture too. They glance at his papers. They thrust them back at him. They point toward Syria. Their mood carries to us on the lingering air. So do their voices.

The man's family stands behind him. A woman, two boys, a teenage girl, bags and belongings piled around their feet. I stare at the teenage girl. She wears a striped cotton tunic and long skirts, a bundle tied across her back with a long scarf. She holds the hand of a small skinny boy. Beneath her bright beaded keffiyeh, her tangle of black matted hair sticks out. I know that hair. The back of my neck prickles. My skin tightens on my bones.

I hardly breathe. "Safaa? Amin?"

My voice is little more than a whisper but she'll hear anyway. My thoughts will reach her from here. I wait for her to turn. To look at me with her dark eyes.

"Sit down, Ghalib," Baba says.

I didn't even know I'd stood up. I whip around to him. "It's Safaa and Amin, Baba. Look!"

With their backs to me, Safaa and Amin watch the man talk to the border guards. I don't need to see their faces. I recognize them instantly. I know how she stands. How he clings to her. Who are these people with them?

"I have her bag," I say. "They don't know we're here."

"Sit down," Baba says again.

His voice has a warning edge to it. That's not important right now. It's more important to tell Safaa and Amin we're here. To get them away from the border with its armed guards and that crazy man with his documents and gestures and pointing.

"I'll get them," I say. "I'll tell them we're here."

"No, Ghalib!" Baba says.

His fingers snatch at my shirt but he's too slow. I slip from his grasp. Step down the slope. I move away from my family.

"Back in a minute," I say.

"Ghalib!" Dayah says.

Heads turn toward me. I'm farther from my family, nearer to Safaa and Amin.

"Come back, Ghalib," Alan says.

My plastic sandals slip and slide over loose pebbles and water bottles. I slither down. Trip over piles of belongings. People stare as I push past. I hear whispers, a sharp intake of breath. In seconds I'm off the slope, moving on the level, closer to the border crossing. Closer to Safaa and Amin.

The border guards hear me, or perhaps they hear the hush in the crowd. Dark suspicion fills their eyes. They watch me. They hold still. Everything holds still. Where before the air was full of talking and shouting and movement, my world is now frozen. I hear only the soft slap of my sandals as though I'm the only person moving.

Maybe this wasn't such a good idea.

I sweat under my shirt. Part of me regrets being here, but a bigger part of me is happy to have found Safaa. I get close to where she stands. I swing the carpetbag off my shoulder to hand it over. The guards' eyes lock on the bag. My world explodes.

Guards hurl themselves against the family, flinging them to the dirt. They swing guns around. Point them at my head. The crowd screams. The raw sound drills into my skull. Amin and Safaa twist around to stare at me. I see their faces. I realize I don't know them at all. The girl isn't Safaa. Older, with pale flat eyes, she looks at me, terrified.

I search her face but can't see any of Safaa's wild-cat stare. The boy is younger, with shorter hair than Amin. He doesn't have a comfort headscarf. He stares at me, at the carpetbag, with frightened eyes. I understand their fear. A moment ago, I was a curiosity. Now I'm a possible suicide bomber with a bag of explosives.

I fling the bag from me, toward the trench and barbed wire. The guards track it with their muzzles. The crack of gunfire splits the air. The explosion of noise deafens me. In a blaze of smoke and bullets, Safaa's bag bursts into a million shreds of carpet and torn clothing and scraps of cloth. The crowd screams and stampedes. I run too, pelting toward the shelter of the canopy. Turkish border guards burst into the sunlight from beneath it, guns pointed, ready to shoot. They catapult toward me, casting their eyes around in search of the suicide bomber. I crash to the dirt. Cover my head. Gasp for forgiveness. Guards pound past me. I pull myself from the ground and look after them. The guards are still running. Still searching for the suicide bomber. They don't realize it was me.

Legs shaking, I take off again. I hammer beneath the canopy. My footsteps echo and repeat in the shadows. Behind me, something pops and whooshes. I hear it again. I look back. The air fills with clouds of white smoke. People gasp. Cough and splutter.

Run from the slopes. They cover their mouths. Two drivers stand at their trucks, staring at the screaming crowds, at the bedlam and the white smoke.

"Tear gas!" one of them says. They clamber into their cabs. Shut the doors.

I run. I leave behind gunfire and screams and stampeding crowds. I leave behind choking white smoke, but even so, it stings my throat, my eyes, my breathing. My lungs burn like fire. I keep running. I burst from the shadows and into the open air and hard sunshine. My feet scald me. I think only of getting away.

Behind me is more gunfire. More screaming. More running. I hear footsteps now. They're after me! Guards are chasing me.

I don't stop. I don't look around. I keep running. My damaged feet pound the road, every step slicing pain through me. The road slopes upward, climbing the flank of a hill. At the top is a rocky outcrop of boulders and loose stones with shrubs and straggling bushes. If I can reach that without a bullet in my back, I might survive. I'll hide. Catch my breath.

Footsteps gain on me, hammering along the road. Closer all the time. Any second I expect a hand to grab me. To drag me to the ground. More than one guard chases me. I hear their gasping breaths, their grunts as they climb the hill. They move fast, but I don't slow down. I keep going, my eyes fixed on the rocks. I can't run much farther. My heart leaps in my chest. My hurt lungs burn. My feet feel as though I'm running on blades. I stumble. Almost fall, but recover.

"Come on, boy," a voice says. "Keep going."

A man is almost alongside me. He's not a guard. He speaks Arabic like a Syrian.

"You've made it this far," he says. "You can reach the rocks." He runs past me.

I glance back. Other people are strung along the length of the road. Nobody is in uniform. Nobody is a border guard. Men. A boy. A woman at the rear. I face forward. My head spins but I run as fast as I can. The rocky outcrop is closer now. I'm nearly there.

I duck between massive boulders. I stop running at last. Lean over, hands on my knees. I throw up, gulping for air. Shuddering retches shake my whole body. My breath rips through my chest.

"Breathe," the man says. "Breathe."

My face and shirt are soaked with tears, or sweat, or vomit. I can't even lift my head. Who is this man? What happened?

"You're through," the man says. He's out of breath too, gasping his words. He smiles. "We're all through. We're safe. They won't chase us this far."

I pull myself upright. Stare at him.

"I don't know what you did," he says, "but you opened a chance for us. We ran on your heels. Through the border. Out of Syria. Into Turkey."

I've crossed the border. I'm in Turkey.

This is where I wanted to go, except I'm not with my family. I'm alone. I have nothing except the clothes on my back.

I scan the sweating faces around me. Everyone smiles. Laughs even. They pant. They wipe hot brows. The woman hugs a man and a teenage boy: she is with family. Giddy relief seems to pass through everyone but me. I didn't plan this. These people are not my family. I know none of them.

"I thought it was Safaa and Amin," I say to the man. It's a stupid thing to say. It makes no sense to anyone but me.

"I said to Ali you didn't look like a suicide bomber," the man says.

He slaps the back of another man propped against the rock, who squints at me in the brightness of the dropping sun.

"You don't look like much at all," says the other man, Ali.

"You know they could have shot you?" the first man says.

I don't know what to say. I didn't mean to do anything. I just wanted to give Safaa her bag. To tell her where we were. Except it wasn't Safaa or Amin. My eyes wanted to see them so much that I believed it was them. My eyes told me lies. Now my heart is breaking because I'm alone on the wrong side of the border.

"Why are you crying?" Ali says. "You're safe now."

"I'm on my own." My voice cracks.

"You're not on your own," he says. "We're here. What's your name?" He puts his hand on my shoulder.

I pull away. Ali and the man with him look perhaps in their twenties. They wear jeans and imitation leather jackets, like the ones in the market in Kobani.

"This is my brother Musab," Ali says. "We're from Aleppo."

"I'm Ghalib," I say at last. I'm a little wary. I wish I wasn't alone. "From Kobani. My family is on the other side of the border."

The border is now empty of people and traffic, but crawling with Turkish guards in gas masks.

The tear gas lingers and drifts like smoke. Buses and trucks move back from the crossing. Horns blare. Engines rev. People shout.

"We need to move," Ali says. He looks at the group. "Backup will arrive any moment from Reyhanli. This place will be crawling with soldiers."

"We're heading for Reyhanli Refugee Camp," says the man with the family. "We'll follow the road."

"Your decision," says Ali. "But a dangerous one. My brother and I will hide in the hills until dark and then follow the road to town."

The family listens. So does another man who ran with us. He hasn't spoken yet. An older man with dark skin, he wears a traditional long robe, skinny legs poking from it. He grips a small bundle and doesn't look strong enough to outrun border guards, yet that's exactly what he did.

A distant scream of sirens swells and fades with the mood of the breeze. Backup is already on its way. I don't want to be on the road when the Turkish army arrives.

"Hills," says the old man to no one in particular. His voice is gruff. Before anyone replies, he's off the highway, climbing the scrubby shale like a skinny goat.

"Come on, Ghalib," says Musab.

I look at him like a fool. I don't know what to do. My chest hurts. My gut is loose. I look at the border where my family is. I look up the steep hillside, where the old man is already well up its flanks. I look along the road to Reyhanli.

"You'll be safer in the hills," says Musab. "You can decide what to do tomorrow."

I climb, grabbing handholds and scrambling over boulders as I follow the two brothers, who clamber ahead of me. In minutes, I emerge from the rocky cluster to find myself already high above the road. A fresh wind whips my hair and cools my cheeks. The stony ground is loose, scattered with small spiky shrubs. Breathless and sweating, I look at the narrow tracks rising steeply up the hillside: old goat trails leading through the barren hills of Turkey. Far ahead, the old man scurries over the trails.

I look back at Syria. Nobody is on the slopes where I spent the whole day with my family. People have retreated from the gunfire and tear gas. I turn my back on the border and follow two strangers through the darkening hills deeper into Turkey.

12

We stop climbing when it gets too dark to see.

"It's dangerous to continue," Musab says.

We crouch among the scrub and loose rocks in a small fold among the fabric of the hills. I'm relieved to stop. My feet burn in my sandals. The ragged bandages Baba wrapped for me are shredded and filthy. My chest gurgles and my throat stings from the tear gas. I look at the sky as the last light leaks from it and the stillness of night settles around.

With a jolt of shock, I realize we're not alone. Loose stones scrape behind me. The crunch of footfall. The rub of clothing. Someone is coming through the dark. Someone who moves without speaking.

I peer through the blackness until my eyes ache. It's too dark to see anything. Who is in these wild hills? Soldiers searching for us?

I see a shadow. I flinch. Ali lunges forward to grab someone in the dark. A boy screams. A woman cries out.

"*As-salamu alaykum!*" a man says. "Don't hurt us!"

It's the man who crossed the border with his family.

Ali grips him around the neck. Holds him tight until he is certain. "Why sneak up on us?" His voice is cold and hard.

"We came up the hillside away from the road," the man says. His voice is tight. Frightened. "We couldn't catch up to you. We didn't know you had stopped."

Ali releases the man. When we've all calmed down and caught our breath, the six of us settle overnight in this barren place. I feel even lonelier now that there are more of us. The brothers and the family chat among themselves, but I am silent. I'm also cold. The breeze has a bite and my damp shirt is chill against my skin. I haven't had anything to eat or drink since morning. I'm not hungry, but all I can think of is water—clean and fresh and running. My throat is dry, my mouth sticky. I long for a bottle of water. Even a mouthful. But there's none. This will be a long night.

The soft talk finally dies down. The night deepens and the others sleep. I alone remain awake. I gaze at the stars, shouting their brightness from the Turkish horizon on one side to the Syrian horizon on the other. I think of Baba and wonder if he's watching the stars too. I think of my family, waiting to cross. I wonder where Safaa and Amin are now, and realize how stupid I was to see them in two strangers. Darkness soaks into my blood like a stain I'll carry forever. I'm so cold, so thirsty, so scared.

Sleep doesn't come. In the cold moonlight, I look at the people around me. The family curls together in a tight knot. Watching them hurts my heart. Musab and Ali also lie close; one of them snores but I can't tell which. I envy their closeness. They're brothers. They have each other's back. There's strength in that. I feel stronger when I'm with Alan and Hamza, and wish more than anything they were with me now. Family means everything. Family feeds my soul. I turn from the group so their togetherness no longer aches my heart.

"You need to watch out, boy," a voice says.

I whip around. The woman watches me from between her men. I'm a little comforted that she's awake, even though she's a stranger. She doesn't move, but her voice is clear and soft. She glances toward Ali and Musab. When she hears them snore, she turns back to me.

"Think about where to go tomorrow," she says. "It's more difficult on your own."

I hold my breath. I nod to let her know I've heard her, but I'm afraid to speak in case my feelings spill out of me and I lose control. We sit in silence until her eyes close. I squeeze my eyes shut to keep out the dark night. I try not to think.

I don't sleep at all. I open my eyes again when the sky pales in the east. There are still stars in the dark side. My eyes are gritty and sore, as though full of sand. My lips are dry and chapped. I'm freezing cold, deep in my bones. I stay as still as possible: as soon as I move, I'll start to shiver and I'm afraid that I won't be able to stop.

The man and his wife are still asleep. Their son nods to me, then stares with red-rimmed eyes at nothing in particular. He looks as wretched as I feel.

Ali and Musab sit together, talking quietly. Musab comes to hunker next to me. His eyes are bloodshot. The corners of his mouth are cracked.

"Your feet are hurt, Ghalib," he says.

135

"I got burned." My voice is dry and strange. I swallow, but my mouth holds no moisture.

"Ali has a scarf," says Musab. "I'll bind them for you before we go. Will you travel on with us today?"

I only want to go back to my family, but I know it's not possible. "Where are you going?"

"Ankara."

I stare at him. "Ankara's far away."

"We won't get there for many days—weeks even—but we have cousins expecting us there."

"My family will look for me when they cross the border," I say.

"Then Ankara is the place to go," says Musab. "Every Syrian heads for Ankara. It's easy to travel to, and a major city. Your family will know to find you there."

I never heard Baba talk about Ankara, but then I never listened when he talked of where we would go in Turkey. I wish Bushra was here. She would remember.

"We can talk about it later," Musab says. "I'll get the scarf for your feet."

We have nothing to eat or drink, and little to carry. As soon as everyone is awake, and my feet are bound, we walk on. I'm scared to travel farther from the border and my family, but I can't stay in the hills another night. I need water, food, warmth. I shiver with cold for the first half hour, until my blood gets moving and the sun crests the hills. We all walk more slowly than yesterday because everyone is tired and thirsty, and there are no guards chasing us. The family is in front, then Ali, while Musab falls into step with me at the back.

"Ali and I work with a resistance movement in Ankara," Musab says. "We fight the Turks." He looks at me. "You're Kurdish?"

There are Syrians who want Kurds to be thrown out of Syria. There are Syrians who blame Kurds for the war, for rebel strikes on schools and hospitals, for lots of bad things happening all over Syria. Sometimes it isn't safe to say you're Kurdish. This might be one of those times.

But Musab doesn't wait for me to answer. He nods as though I've already replied. Maybe he understands why I say nothing.

"We work with Syrian Kurds," he says. "Members of the People's Protection Units."

This is news to me. Why would soldiers like Mahmoud and Dima want to go to Ankara? There's so much work for them in Kobani. In Syria.

"Kurds are everywhere." Musab says it like it's a good thing. "You could work with us too. Help your people to build the resistance."

Ali joins us.

"Turkey sends airstrikes to bomb Syrian Kurds," he says. "Did you know that?"

I don't reply right away. I get confused about who's sending planes and helicopters and airstrikes and barrel bombs. It seems to change every day. Inside Syria, there are rebel groups and pro-government soldiers and regional forces. Outside Syria, lots of different countries are involved: Russia and the UK, Saudi Arabia and France, Iran, the United States. And now Turkey.

"I think so," I say at last. Bushra would be furious if she heard my hesitant tone. I hear her voice in my head, chiding me for not knowing better.

"Our resistance movement fights Turkish plans to bomb Syria," Ali says. "Some of our brothers have already gone to Ankara."

Musab and Ali remind me of Dima and Mahmoud. If I refuse to go with them, will they cut my throat?

"I'm only thirteen," I say.

"You're strong and brave—we saw that yesterday when you broke through the border," Musab says.

"I'm *not* strong or brave." I want to say I'm frightened and confused. I wish yesterday had never happened.

"We need boys like you to run messages and deliver information to help Syria," Ali says. "In time, we would teach you to do more important work."

"You'll be safe with us," Musab says. "You'll have somewhere safe to sleep and good food."

I need somewhere safe to sleep, instead of an empty hillside with no shelter. My belly rumbles at the mention of food. This is a generous offer. I don't have any other choices.

"What about my family?"

"As soon as your family arrives, you're free to go with them," Ali says. "You're young. You need your family. But until they get here, you can stay with us. We'll teach you skills to fight the Turks."

At last we reach a place where the goat trail winds close to the main road. We decide to continue on the empty road. A steep channel drops down from the trail. The family man is first to clamber down. He slips on loose dirt and gravel. He snatches at rocks and weeds. He slides and blunders down a vertical part, finally stumbling out at the roadside. He waves his wife forward.

If the man was awkward, his wife is ten times worse. It takes her half a dozen tries to even get going. She grabs her son's hand as she takes her first step and almost pulls him after her. She slips and tumbles. She gives a little shriek. I think she's going to crash headfirst, but she plonks herself onto the dirt and slides down on her backside in a cloud of dust and a scattering of pebbles. The man helps her to her feet. She brushes off the dirt and rearranges her scarf. When his turn comes, their son takes long strides. He even manages to keep his balance at the last straight-down part and to end with a run.

It's my turn. I stand at the top of the cutting. It's steep and long, ending at a narrow bend between rocks, then that short vertical drop. My heart skips a beat. My head is light and my lips are dry.

"Come on, boy," says the family man. "We don't have all day." I flicker my gaze toward him. Impatience is etched on his face.

I keep my balance for the first part, grabbing weeds and bushes. Thorns pierce beneath my nails. Shale is loose under my feet. Then the scarf on my feet slides inside my sandals. I'm out of control. I slither and crash. I slam into the rock face. The ground beneath me drops away and I plummet. I cry out.

My shout is cut short by a thud that knocks me senseless.

– – –

"Open your eyes, Ghalib," a voice says.

I'm lying on gravel at the side of the road. The sun dazzles. Musab looks down at me.

"He's alive," he says.

His voice sounds like he is speaking through a tunnel. My belly is sick. My face feels like it's been pounded with rocks. Musab helps me sit up. He hands me a cloth to press to my bloody nose and split lip. My head throbs with its own heartbeat.

"Take your time," he says. "You knocked your-self out."

I look at my scraped knuckles. My jeans are torn, and through the gaping holes I see grazed shins. The rest of the group sits in the shade, watching. They say nothing, but the woman nods and I realize the cloth I'm holding to my nose is a headscarf. She must have given me a spare one. Musab helps me clamber to my feet. The family man stands up.

"We move on," he says.

I stumble after them. The woman hovers close by and, though she doesn't say anything, I like having her near. Musab and Ali walk ahead with the man and his son. We stay in the shade whenever possible, as the sun is high and hot. My lips are parched; the split has dried and cracked. My mouth feels swollen. Reyhanli seems such a long way away. Every step is tougher. I stumble over rocks and brush. I feel dizzy and sick.

Slowly, the hills around us change their shape and fabric.

There are crops, animals grazing on the slopes, workers in distant fields. We pass small sheds off the side of the road. Farm tools and sacks of feed lean against the walls.

"We need water," Ali says.

He finds a little well behind of one of the small-holdings where clear water trickles into a stone trough. We scoop it into our hands. Water has never tasted so sweet and looked so bright. I drink until my belly aches. I sluice its coldness over my face, clean off the dried blood, wet my cracked lips. The water stings my knuckles. I rinse out the woman's scarf and offer it to her.

"Keep it," she says.

I soak the scarf and hang it around my neck. As we leave the yard, my world has steadied again. We see locals working in the fields who straighten up to stare at us. We pass holdings and farmhouses, dogs that bark and take little runs to scare us off their territory. The family throws stones at them. We pass a group of children who throw stones at us. We round a bend in the road and, in the distance, the Syrian flag flaps and fights in a warm breeze curving down the valley. I stare. I rub my gritty eyes. We're in Turkey yet here is my country's flag flying high and proud.

"Reyhanli Refugee Camp," the family man says.

At a junction on the road, a rusted signpost points left to Reyhanli. On a plank of wood propped on the dirt bank, someone has painted *Little Syria*. An arrow points right. The family man looks at the brothers.

"This is where we separate," he says. He bids me farewell: "*Ma'a as-salaama.*"

Ali and Musab shake hands with the man and his son; they smile and nod respectfully at the woman. Musab beckons me with a jerk of his head. I don't move. The family man doesn't hold out his hand to me, but he watches. He says nothing. Many words that have never found their way to his lips are written in his eyes. He waits.

I don't know what to do or where to go. This is too difficult a decision. To stay near the border in the refugee camp with strangers? To travel hundreds of miles to a distant city with Musab and Ali? The brothers offered me food and shelter, but how will my family know I'm in Ankara? This man, his wife and son have hardly spoken to me, but they're family. Not *my* family, but *a* family. The woman gave me her scarf when I was bleeding. Her words during the dark night come back to me now: *Think about where to go tomorrow. It's more difficult on your own.*

Dayah's words jump into my head too: *Why can't you keep your head about you, Ghalib?* Hamza would have no problem jumping to a decision: he would travel to Ankara in a heartbeat. But I don't want to travel to a city in a strange country when my family is behind in Syria. They're so close. So strong in my heart.

I finally turn to Ali and Musab. I hold out my hand. "*Allah yusallmak,*" I say. "Thank you for your kindness."

My voice sounds thick. I don't know if it's from my swollen face or because feelings inside me threaten to leak out. Ali shakes my hand and walks away. He says nothing. He doesn't look back. Musab holds my hand for a brief moment. He looks into my eyes.

"I thought you would fight with us for Syria, Ghalib," he says. "You would make a good soldier."

He runs to catch up with his brother.

The man waits for me. "You made a brave decision," he says.

I walk with him and his family toward the refugee camp. I say nothing. A rush of warmth fills me but, even so, my head and my heart battle with each other for the next hour while we walk in silence. I can't stop wondering if I've made the right decision.

The camp is set low in a valley, a vast spread of tents in endless rows and clusters. Many are printed with a crescent moon on their canvas roofs. As well as tents, there are metal shipping containers and makeshift lean-tos, caravans, tarpaulin shelters.

"Syrians are here?" I say.

"Only Syrians," the man says.

My heart sinks when I see the rows of high metal fencing topped with barbed wire surrounding the camp. It's like the border again. Like the armed and barbed barricade that stops my family from being with me.

"What if they won't let us in?" I say. My voice is small. Terror rushes through me. I can't face another night of dense cold in my bones, of dark loneliness in my heart.

"They'll let us in," the man says.

A guard at the main gate stops us. The family man explains that I'm traveling alone, that he is with his family. We're directed toward a shipping container where people sort papers and work at tables stacked with documents and boxes. We're issued a number and join other families and new arrivals waiting outside. I sit on the dusty ground. I hurt all over. My feet feel again as though I've been walking on knives. Blood stains the strips of scarf. Once again, all I think of is water to drink.

It's early evening when our turn comes. The sky is already dusky blue and long shadows stretch across the ground. Inside, the official looks tired. She sweats in her headscarf. She turns first to me.

"You are an unaccompanied minor?" she says.

I blink at her. My head can't find an answer.

"Are you alone?" she says.

"Yes. I'm alone." The words stick in my throat. I almost cry.

And now the official does something I never

expected: she smiles at me. I stare at her. This is the first time anyone has smiled at me since I came into Turkey.

"We take care of unaccompanied minors," she says. "Boys and girls like you who are traveling alone. Don't be afraid. We'll look after you."

Her kindness overwhelms me and opens the darkness in my heart. Tears rush to my eyes and down my cheeks. I turn away. I try to mop my tears with the grubby scarf, but they won't stop leaking from my eyes. I didn't realize I had so much water still inside me. Through my sobs, I hear the official's words.

"It's fine to be upset," she says. "This is Mohammad. He'll take you to the clinic first, and then the children's center."

Through my tears, I see a young man with a red armband beside the official. He also smiles and gestures for me to follow him. I wobble a bit as I stand, but my legs find their strength. I nod my good-bye to the family and we head off.

Mohammad has plenty to talk about as he marches me through the camp, though his friendly words wash over me. I have no idea where we're going. Everything is a blur. Everything is frightening. We pass so many tents, some with makeshift shelters and tarpaulin sheeting. Groups of people, families, stare as we pass. A man squats beside a pool of muddy water, plucking a chicken. Two kids throw stones at a rat. Teenage boys build a shelter from sticks and sheets of plastic. Diggers and tractors sit alongside heaps of ripped-up earth and sacks of building materials.

"We're expanding the camp," Mohammad says. "We need more space."

My head is too full with everything. My legs won't move how I want them to. My world spins. I stumble. Try to catch myself. Crash to the ground. Mohammad rushes to my side. He takes my arm, lifts me to my feet.

"I'll help you," he says. "We're nearly at the clinic."

The clinic is a white shipping container surrounded by medical tents. The smell of diesel smoke from the shipping container's generator reminds me strongly of home. Even though it's almost dark, people crowd around outside. Mohammad helps me to a chair at the entrance. Three doctors work in white coats with sleeves rolled up. Boxes of medicines are stacked on racks, more on the floor. It smells like Baba's pharmacy. In a good way, it reminds me of home. Mohammad fetches a doctor, who sits next to me. "What is your name?" he says. He has white skin and a foreign accent. He smells of lemons. It's a nice smell.

"Ghalib," I say.

"How old are you, Ghalib?"

"Thirteen."

As he talks, the doctor's hands skim over my face, my arms, my head. His eyes search my bruised and cut face. He takes a long strip of colored paper and wraps it around my upper arm. He writes notes on his pad.

"When did you last eat, Ghalib?"

"I don't know."

"Your last drink of water?"

My head is fuzzy. When did we stop at the water trough? "Earlier today, I think. Maybe yesterday."

He listens to my breathing with his stethoscope. He looks closely at me.

"Your chest is not good," he says. "What happened?"

"Barrel bomb."

His fingertips touch the lump on my forehead, my split lip. He sees Ali's torn dressings on my feet. "And these?"

"Same bomb."

I bite my lip as he unknots the bloody strips. The stench of infection rises before he finishes. I stare at my raw and oozing feet.

"We need to treat these," he says. "You'll have to stay with us for a while, Ghalib, so we can get you into better shape. Mohammad will bring you something to eat. You can rest, build yourself up. How does that sound?"

His face breaks into a smile. Once again, stupid tears spill down my cheeks. I turn away, ashamed in front of this foreign doctor. I'm too old to cry but I can't seem to stop.

13

I don't know where I am. I'm too scared to look. I lie with my eyes squeezed shut and listen for clues.

There are footsteps close by. The clink of bottles or jars. In the distance, I hear voices. I lie on something soft and comfortable. It wraps me in its curving sides and smells of canvas and outdoors and heat. There are other smells too: medicine and antiseptic, like Baba's pharmacy. Food cooking. A soft breeze blows across my cheeks. I breathe its coolness. I open my eyes.

I lie on a narrow camp bed with a wooden frame. The roof of a tent high above presses and lifts with gusts of wind. The flaps at the open doorway billow in and out, cooling the heat-heavy air.

I'm in the clinic in the refugee camp in Turkey. I'm alone. The light in the tent is twilight blue.

Evening. I must have slept through last night and all of today after seeing the foreign doctor. Almost twenty-four hours! Dayah always says I love my sleep.

I pull myself to a sitting position. I need to pee. I swing my legs to the side but my aching head doesn't like the movement. I sit for a moment for the rolling sickness to settle. I look at the clean bandages on my feet, the fresh T-shirt I wear.

"It's good to see you're awake, Ghalib," a woman says. She crosses the tent and smiles as though she knows me. I have no idea who she is. I can't even concentrate enough to greet her.

"I need the toilet," I say.

"I'll bring you a bottle."

I stare at her, horrified. I will not pee into a bottle in front of this woman. "I can use a toilet." I try to stand. Dizziness grips me and I sit again.

"Give yourself time," the woman says. "You've been asleep for two days."

Two days. I've slept for two whole days!

The woman puts a cardboard bottle on the bed and wheels a screen around to give me privacy. When I'm finished, she pulls back the screens. She examines the dressings on my feet, and other cuts and bruises. She listens to my breathing.

"All good," she says. "Even your chest has cleared."

My head aches and my body feels stiff and heavy. It must be from being in bed too long.

"You've got some color today," she says. "The doctor will want to see you now that you're awake, but you'll be here for a while yet." She brings me sweet tea, fried bread, and a bottle of water.

I feel stronger after eating but still drowsy. I lie on my camp bed. I remember someone helping to wash the dirt and dust off me, the pain when they cleaned and dressed my burned feet, but not much more. I think of my family and wonder where they are. Before long, I'm asleep again.

The pain in my heart, like a dark hole, wakes me with a shock. Dayah and Baba, Bushra, Alan and Dapir leap into my thoughts. I lie still. I think I'm having a heart attack—but soon realize the pain comes from missing my family. They're all I think about. All I dream about.

It's morning and a male nurse is on duty. He helps me to a toilet tent outside.

"I'll walk back myself," I say.

The morning air is fresh. I splash my face with cold water and return to my camp bed. The sharp pain in my heart dulls to an ache, though my thoughts are still full of my family. When the doctor arrives, I remember his foreign voice and nice smell.

"You're looking better," he says. "Have you eaten? Are you drinking lots of water? Have you used the toilet?"

He seems satisfied with my answers. He talks to the nurse, studies my file. "A few more days," he says. "Then you can go to the children's center."

After he leaves, the nurse changes my bandages. "Your feet look better," he says. "The blisters are healing and the infection has cleared up."

Mohammad brings eggs and bread and cheese, and a mug of hot sweet tea. I demolish everything and would eat more, but there's nothing left.

"Nothing wrong with your appetite," Mohammad says. He tears open a plastic pack of clothing. "I had to guess your size but I think these will fit."

He hands me a tracksuit, underwear, lace-up trainers, a warm quilted jacket, a woolly hat. I stare at him. "For me?"

The clothes are brand-new. Never worn. They smell of plastic wrapping. I pick up the tracksuit. Red, with white stripes down the legs—the Syrian team colors.

"The national soccer strip?" I say.

Mohammad smiles. "Everything from the Red Crescent is red, so it might be a coincidence."

I don't think so. Alan would love it. I put on the bottoms. They're way too big—nearly an adult size—but I don't care.

"You'll grow into them," Mohammad says.

I tie the cord tight; the pants hang on my hips. The trainers are white. Even the soles. Spotless. Straight from the factory.

"I've never worn closed-in shoes before."

"You can't actually wear them until the bandages are off your feet," Mohammad points out.

There's a blanket and a towel, plus a zip-up plastic bag with soap, comb, razor, toothbrush and washcloth. Mohammad peers at my face. "You probably don't need the razor yet. You can swap it for something else. All the kids do."

He holds up a plastic bowl.

"You'll use this for everything," he says. "Washing, water, food, carrying things. Keep it safe."

– – –

The doctor discharges me three days later, on the condition I return daily to have my dressings changed and breathing monitored. Mohammad walks me to the children's center.

I wear my old sandals until my bandages can be removed. I hold my head high and check that people notice the Syrian national strip I wear. Plenty of others are wearing it too.

"Lots of Syrian soccer supporters here," I say.

Mohammad smiles. Maybe he'll get Alan a Syrian soccer tracksuit when he gets here, but a smaller size. "Every section in camp has its own toilets, kitchens and food center," Mohammad says. "There's a school too."

"School?" It's been so long since I went to school.

"You'll attend once you're strong enough," Mohammad says.

We pass shipping containers, caravans, metal huts with awnings, tents and a handful of concrete buildings. What looked ordered before now seems chaotic and random. Rubbish and food wrappers lodge in every corner. Torn plastic bags snag on poles and awnings. We cross a bridge of old planks laid over thick sludge oozing through the camp. It stinks of sewage and rot.

"Green River," Mohammad says. "*Never* fall in."

The toilets are in a wooden hut. They reek. People stand in line on the saturated ground, waiting to fill buckets, basins and containers from a row of taps on the outside timber wall. A woman squats in the dirt to wash a squawking baby in a metal bucket.

"Drinking water outside," Mohammad says. "Washing water inside."

Webs of cables fasten the tents to pegs hammered into the dirt. Three men drive wooden poles into the ground to hang sheets of plastic on. A shop made from blue tarpaulin sells fried potatoes and falafel, bowls of rice, and sweet tea. Men hunker down outside to eat and talk. At the back of a truck, people in reflective jackets carry boxes of vegetables, sacks of food and bags of flour into a large tent.

"Food center," Mohammad says. "Families collect rations here and cook in the kitchens."

The kitchens are a row of gas burners and open grills set on a concrete slab beneath a sheet of corrugated metal. They're full of women and kids preparing vegetables, frying potatoes and chopping cucumbers.

"You'll eat in the canteen with the other kids in the center," Mohammad says.

The children's center turns out to be a row of four shipping containers surrounded by a broken fence. Little kids play a noisy game with a softball, organized by two women with whistles. Mohammad leads me into the first container. It's crammed with cots and small mattresses. The floor is covered with mats, rugs and scraps of carpet, in the middle of which sits a woman surrounded with papers and documents. Her headscarf is neatly held in place with a fancy pin. She has polished fingernails and gold rings

"I'm Fatima," she says. "I run the children's center."

Fatima helps me fill in a form all about me: my age, date of birth, full name.

"Tell me about your family," she says.

"How did you get separated?" she says.

"How many of you were traveling together?" she says.

She measures me against a paper strip stuck to the wall, asks me to describe the clothes I wore when I arrived.

"When your family crosses over, they'll come here first to find you," Fatima says. "They all look here for lost children. We keep a database to make it easier for everyone."

Musab told me all families head to Ankara to find separated relatives. Musab was wrong. I'm relieved I came here. I doubt that anyone in Ankara would take my name, my date of birth, my height, to help my family find me.

"My lost toddlers sleep in this container," Fatima says. "The next one is for my handful of girls, and the last two for my boys."

Fatima shows me a mattress in the last container. "This is your place now, Ghalib. Your belongings will be safe here."

I look around the container. At the mattress. I hug my new belongings close. "I'll keep them for now."

Fatima smiles at me. "The teenagers are at school," she says. "You'll meet them at lunch."

I'm a little nervous about meeting the others. I'm a lot nervous about going to school. My head is too full of everything new, everything different, to concentrate. My heart is too sore for my family.

Fatima and Mohammad go back to their work, and the morning drags. I sit on my own in the doorway of the container to watch the ball game. Alan would enjoy this, even though he would probably be the slowest player and spend half the time tripping over his own feet.

Dapir and Dayah would help to take care of the little ones if they were here. Bushra would figure out some ingenious way to improve the drainage around the toilets.

By the time I smell lunch cooking on the gas

burners in the kitchens, I'm hungry and fed up and already dreading the long afternoon ahead.

The aroma of food wafts toward us as we walk to the canteen tent. Inside, Mohammad checks names off his list, and I help him to load trays with bowls of vegetable stew and bring them to the table.

"Get yourself a bowl, Ghalib," Mohammad says. "I'll introduce you to the others."

I follow Mohammad to where a large group of older children and teenagers sit wolfing down dishes of stew. There's little chat.

"This is Ghalib," Mohammad says. "Be nice to him—he's just arrived."

A few people lift their heads. Most ignore me. An older boy shifts over to let me sit down. I bend my head to eat. Scan the table as Mohammad checks faces and names and has a quick word with a couple of teenagers.

At the far end of the table, a girl raises her head to stare at me. There's no mistaking that wild frizz of hair, tied back with a bright beaded keffiyeh. I lock on her dark eyes.

I drop my spoon with a clatter; hers freezes midway to her mouth. My heart thunders in my chest as our eyes lock. It's Safaa.

14

White rage rushes through me. It scorches my blood and sears my thoughts. Because of *her*, I'm here. Because of *her*, I'm alone.

If she hadn't disappeared, I would still be with Dayah and Baba and Alan. With Bushra and Dapir. Yet here she sits, at my table, sharing the same food. I push my bowl away.

My breathing rushes fast and shallow. My heart thunders behind my rib cage. I'm furious that she's here. But another emotion surges above my anger: I'm *relieved* she's safe. I shouldn't feel relief for her. I should feel *nothing* for her. She ruined my life. I don't know what to think.

Safaa watches me closely with the same wildness as before. I see anger flash in her eyes, but beneath it, a shadow of fear clouds her gaze. Her eyes flicker to the left. Tucked among the other students is little Amin. He hasn't noticed me. He scoops up his stew, slopping it on the table as he struggles to eat from a too-big spoon. Seeing him is like seeing Alan again. My heart aches. My anger softens. A turmoil of emotions churns through me. I grip the tabletop with white knuckles.

"Ghalib." Mohammad's voice cuts through my thoughts.

I snap my gaze to him. He looks at my pushed-away bowl. Stares at my face. I turn away from him. Other students look at me now. My face burns. I stand up. Step away from the table. Safaa doesn't move, but her black eyes follow me. I can't read her expression.

"I thought she was my friend," I say to Mohammad. "Now I can't even look at her."

I stride outside.

Mohammad jogs alongside me. He looks back. "Who?"

"Safaa." Anger flashes through my words. "It's her fault. She's why I'm here. I was looking for her when everything happened. I thought she wanted to be with my family, but she left us."

My words trip over themselves and drown in my tears.

"Breathe easy," Mohammad says, just like Baba. "Take your time."

I dash away my tears as we walk. I tell Mohammad everything: about Safaa shooting at us and Amin being sick and Baba helping. About arriving at the border, and Safaa's carpet bag, and the guards shooting at me. About sprinting alone across the border. I even tell him about the brothers, Musab and Ali, who wanted me to go to Ankara. Somewhere along the way, my tears stop. I gulp for air. At last I run out of things to say. We're quiet for a while, except I hiccup every so often.

"Everyone who arrives here has been through hell," Mohammad says. "Kids on their own have been through more than most. They don't have parents or aunts or uncles to keep them safe and make decisions with them. Some kids have seen their families killed by airstrikes, or get sick and die. We don't know what they've gone through. Safaa and Amin have only been here for a few days."

He stops walking. I wait to hear what he's going to say. "They haven't spoken at all since they arrived."

"*Nothing?*"

"I didn't even know their names until you told me just now," Mohammad says. "I don't know where

163

they came from. I don't know what language they speak."

"They speak Armenian, I think," I say. "But Arabic too."

Safaa and Amin didn't speak much with my family, but they did speak. Safaa especially was beginning to open up a little more. One part of me wants to help, but I'm still so angry.

"You need to talk to her," Mohammad says.

"I can't."

"It will help both of you."

"I don't need help."

"It would be good to have a friend in the camp."

"She's no friend of mine."

"She did no harm other than leaving without telling you," Mohammad says.

"She shot at us." I sound like Alan when he squabbles with his little friends.

"That's not why you're angry."

Mohammad is right.

"I'll help you," he says. "You must talk to Safaa, or this will eat you up from inside."

I can't go back to the children's center when Safaa is there. I can't leave this camp.

"I don't know what to say."

"Words will come," Mohammad says. "Just promise to try."

"I'll try."

Mohammad claps me on the back. "Great. Let's go."

"Where?"

"To talk to Safaa."

"*Now?*" I'm not ready yet. "What about tomorrow?"

"Now," Mohammad says. "Or you'll spend your time afraid you'll bump into her."

"I'm not afraid," I say. "I'm angry."

"Sometimes they're the same thing."

The other kids are back in school, so Mohammad collects Safaa from class.

"Let's walk," Mohammad says to the two of us.

Safaa's beaded keffiyeh is pulled across her face so I can't see her expression. She looks ready to bolt at any moment and keeps looking behind us, as though checking how far we've come from the school. How far she is from Amin. She probably wishes now that she'd kept her gun and bullets.

Mohammad walks between us, but gradually he pulls back. He tries to be subtle but it's really obvious. I flash him a look; he ignores me.

"How is Amin?" I say at last. It's a beginning.

Safaa says nothing. We won't get far if I'm the only one to do the talking. We walk a little more.

"He's well," she says at last. Her voice is so soft, I doubt Mohammad hears her—I'm right beside her and I hardly hear her. "He wants to see you."

"You told him I'm here?"

"Yes."

"He looks strong."

She doesn't reply, but the wildness she wore isn't so wild now. She isn't so twitchy.

"I looked for you at the border," I say.

I want to say more. I want to shout at her. To tell her I was worried and confused when they vanished. And angry. But maybe it's not time for that yet. I'm working hard to keep my anger from boiling over, but maybe Safaa is working hard too. Words are difficult for her. I listen with every part of me.

"We couldn't sleep," she says. "The smells. The noise. The cold."

"You took your bag."

"I wouldn't leave it for you to carry."

"But not your carpet bag." I don't add that this was the bag that almost got me shot to pieces.

"It was under your mother's head. She was asleep."

I never thought of that. We stop walking.

"We left quietly," she says.

"Why cross without us?"

She shrugs. "Nothing was planned. It happened."

How can you cross a border between countries and not plan it? *How?* Anger rises in me again like black water, but I stop suddenly. I realize that's exactly what happened to me. I never planned to cross the border, yet here I am in Turkey.

"They opened the border for trucks and buses," Safaa says. "A man shouted to us from a bus. We ran fast. He pulled us on—hid us under seats. The guards counted passengers but didn't search. We got off in Reyhanli. We walked here."

I stare at Safaa. Mohammad stares at Safaa. Safaa stops talking. She looks bewildered from saying so much.

Her leaving wasn't planned. It wasn't meant to be this way. My anger is gone. In its place is understanding and a lingering sadness.

"Can I see Amin?" I say.

15

A week later, the nurse removes the bandages from my feet. I come straight back to the children's center and put on my new white trainers. I pull the laces tight and stand up. They feel weird. My feet are shut in. My plastic sandals let my toes wriggle, but there's no space for toe-wriggling in these. I walk outside to show Safaa and Amin. I'm springy. Taller. In pain.

"They look too tight," Safaa says.

"They're perfect," I say. Mohammad might take them back if they don't fit.

My toes are cramped, stiff, but these are new trainers. *New. Trainers.* I'll get used to them. I'll wear them even if they cut the feet off me. I look down at my European feet.

The next day, I start at camp school. I walk light and bouncy, mostly so dust doesn't settle on my shoes, but also because it's the least painful way to walk. When I get there, I see other boys in their trainers, with the laces loose and the tongues folded down. I do the same. It's much more comfortable when my feet aren't strangled.

School here isn't like real school. Students wander in and out all day. Some come for a few days, then stop. Then return. Others, like Safaa and Amin and me, are there every day because Mohammad and Fatima make sure every child in the children's center attends school. Kids from different backgrounds and parts of Syria all cram into the tent. We speak different dialects and have learned different subjects. Everyone has missed some schooling. We mostly write stories about our experiences and memories. The little ones paint pictures and sing songs. Alan would love it, but Bushra would be frustrated because there's so little learning.

I was at the top of my class in Kobani, with plans to study pharmacy in university. Now I can't even concentrate. The teacher is kind and patient. He tells me to write down how I feel and what I'm thinking, but I'm afraid to start. I have so many feelings I'm afraid I won't be able to stop writing. I don't want to put my thoughts down on paper. I don't want

to show them to anyone. It's safer to hide them—
then they don't seem so real. I think of my family
instead. I look at every boy Alan's age and think of
my brother. I even look at every girl Bushra's age and
think of my sister. I miss everything about Syria: my
house, my friends, my aunts and uncles, my cousins.
I even miss the streets and the markets. I miss the
shops and the bunch of little kids who played on our
street, lining up stones and pebbles. But most of all,
I miss my family. I don't sleep at night. I lie on my
mattress and think of Dayah and Baba and Dapir. I
wonder how Hamza is doing back in Kobani. I wish
I was still with him.

Once school is finished, there's little to do. I
don't talk much with the other boys. I'm the Kurdish
outsider. Safaa, Amin and I walk around the camp,
sometimes talking, mostly just walking. Several
times, we see the family I crossed the border with. I
nod at them but we don't talk.

The boys in my container tease me about walking with Safaa.

"You're too old to walk together," they say.

"Have you found your wife?" they say.

"She should have a male relative with her,"
they say.

"Amin is her brother," I say. "He fulfills the role."

One afternoon, we cross the wooden planks laid over the stinking green ooze. At the barber's tent, I trade my razor for a haircut. Safaa waits outside. Amin stands next to me to watch at close range. The barber holds up the long strands of hair curling down the nape of my neck.

"Short?" he says.

"Short."

When I come out, Safaa covers her mouth and turns away so I don't see her laughter. Her shoulders shake. I finger the short stubble on my scalp.

"Is it that bad?"

"It has to last," she says. "You don't have another razor."

We walk back to the children's center. The wind is cool on my scalp. I put my hand up to feel the shape of my skull beneath the fuzz.

"It'll grow," Safaa says.

Back at the children's center, Fatima laughs. "What have you done to yourself?"

"Haircut," I say.

"What will they think?" she says.

"Who?"

"The family waiting for you at reception."

I stop. I stare at her. I hardly dare to say the words. "My family?"

Fatima laughs again. "They arrived this afternoon. Go quick now."

I walk out of the children's center. It's like stepping into a different world. A rarer world. A bigger world. The sky tilts and stretches above me. Ground shadows yawn wide and dark and thrilling. The hairs on my shorn scalp tingle like electricity runs through them. Amin stares at me, but I don't stop. Safaa calls my name, but I can't talk. Every part of me urges me on, aching with hunger. Driving me toward reception. I pick up my pace, jogging over the dusty ground. My toes feel every dip and yield on the path, even through the soles of my trainers. Little puffs of dirt rise in whispers and hushes beneath my feet. Bright air slides over my cheeks, hot and dry. As I sprint faster, the layers I've built to protect myself since I crossed the border flake off, like scorched leaves on the trees along Kobani's Aleppo Way. They drift to the bare earth like a thousand feathers, memories of my terror and aloneness and cold dark nights, until I'm left bare. Raw. Exposed. None of me is hidden anymore. My feelings are on show for all to see. They shine wet on my face. They tremble in my bones, my muscles, my gleaming blood.

Reception is in front of me. Dayah stands next to it. My Dayah. Darkness lifts from my blood and my heart sings. I see her before she sees me. She watches every child passing by, her face pale and haunted. A twist of guilt tightens my belly. I've caused so much pain by leaving my family and crossing into Turkey alone. And I'll be in trouble for nearly getting shot dead by border guards. I stop running. I hold still for a heartbeat. I want to keep the sweetness of this moment captured in my memory for ever. Until now, I didn't know how frightened I was.

Dayah sees me. She freezes, eyes locked on mine. "Ghalib! My Ghalib."

Her voice is a whisper, but a whisper with a burning edge to it. Everything releases inside me. I run into her outstretched arms and she snatches me to her. She runs her hands over me, feeling the shape of my skull with her fingertips, my arms and legs. The curve of my spine. The wings of my shoulders. I'm too old for her to do this, but I don't care. I. Don't. Care. Her consuming love is like flowers blossoming over my fears. Building up layers of protection again. We cry. We laugh.

Only when she's certain I'm uninjured does

Dayah hug me tightly to her, gripping me like she'll never let me go. She presses her face to the top of my head. I hear her breath above me, her heartbeat against mine. She pushes me back to look at me fully.

"Oh, Ghalib!" she says. "What happened?" Her fingers explore the fresh stubble on my scalp. "Lice or fleas?"

"I traded my razor."

"You asked for this?" Her eyes fill with wonder.

"Economy cut."

"But you have nothing left, Ghalib. Let's hope it grows fast." She draws her fingertip down my cheek. "But my first son is alive and well." Her searching fingers pluck the shoulder of my new tracksuit. "New clothes?"

"Is everyone well?" I say.

She traces the seam of my T-shirt, straightening it across my shoulders. "How are your poor burned feet?"

"When did you cross the border?"

So many questions hang in the air. So many lost answers. Her eyes look at my laced trainers, still clean-looking. Still new. I've taken good care of them. Her gaze slides up to my face.

"Where are the others?" I say. "Alan? Baba?"

Her face changes.

"What?" My heart tightens like a claw grips it. Now is the time for truths to be told.

"They're in the clinic," she says.

My world shrivels again. The tilting sky plummets. Shadows lose their immense and wondrous shapes. The urge is still in me, stronger now, burning me up.

"I know where the clinic is."

"Wait," Dayah says.

I grab her hand. Drag her toward the clinic. We hurry past shelters, the wooden toilet hut. The kitchens. The food centers. Dayah pulls back a little. Slows me down.

"The foreign doctor will help," I say.

"Slow down," Dayah says.

We pass diggers and tractors tearing up the earth, expanding the camp.

"He speaks good Arabic. He smells nice. We're almost there," I say.

The clinic is crowded with patients and familiar smells and medics I recognize. My eyes search for Baba. Bushra. Dapir. Most of all for Alan.

There they are! There they are! I breathe again. I'm complete.

Baba is talking with the doctor, Bushra next to him. She looks different somehow. Newer. I've never felt such happiness to see my sister. My *sister*! But she isn't the one I'm looking for. Bushra startles when she sees me. I pass her. Sense her reach for me, hear my name on her lips.

"Ghalib—" Baba says.

Not now. Not yet. There is Alan. He lies on a camp bed like mine. His eyes are closed, dark shadows beneath them. He's paler than I've ever seen him. I take in the familiar bend of his gimpy leg, the little curled left hand.

"Alan," I say.

He doesn't answer. Doesn't move. His eyelashes tremble like the wings of tiny insects. I kneel beside him.

"Baba?" I say.

"He'll be fine, Ghalib," Baba says. He puts his hand on my shoulder. "The doctor will make him better. It's dehydration. Exhaustion. Nothing more."

Baba helps me to my feet and smiles. It's a smile of truth. A dam-burst of fireworks explodes in my chest. It floods me with something I can't explain. Like soap bubbles. Like blue sky. Like shooting stars. It tastes of home and shining and fire all at once. I can't speak. Baba leads me outside.

"Let the doctors care for him," he says. "We'll visit later." We're surrounded by sunshine. Brightness in the air and lightness in my heart. I breathe. My heart slows. Baba hugs me close, whispers his love in my ear. Dayah smiles. Bushra pinches me on the arm. I hug her.

"You're so brave," she says. I pull back to look in her eyes. I see only honesty there. I believe her.

A lot is happening. Much to take in. I look around. Peer past Dayah and Baba. There's one person missing. I search faces, eyes, expressions. I don't see the answer I'm looking for. Blackness rises through me again, rinsing away the brightness in my blood.

"Dapir?"

"I tried to tell you," Dayah says. Her whisper burns with pain. "I didn't want you to find out this way, Ghalib."

I shake my head as though I might shake the truth away. The truth I already know. "No, Dayah." Tears spring to my eyes.

"She was old," Baba says. "The journey was too much for her. She got sick."

"But your medicines." My words break with my heart. "You could fix her."

"I couldn't fix her heartache," Baba says.

"Was it me?" I whisper. I'm afraid of the answer. Afraid to breathe. "Did I cause her heartache?"

"No, Ghalib." Baba pulls me close. "War broke Dapir's heart. She couldn't leave her homeland. It was too much for her."

"Where is she now?" I say.

"In Syrian soil," Baba says. "Where she would have wanted."

"She never left Syria?"

"She never wanted to leave Syria."

"She was peaceful when she died," Dayah says.

Everything just given to me has been snatched away again. The hardness of the camp, the coldness of the dark night, the death of Dapir, all slam through me like a barrel bomb, ripping my heart to pieces. I sob. Baba holds me.

"This is all my fault."

"None of it is your fault, Ghalib," Baba says. "Not Dapir's death. Not Hamza's injuries. Not crossing the border, Ghalib. Always remember that."

"I want go back in time to before the war," I say. "I want to go home."

16

Mohammad promises Alan a tracksuit if he eats his food and builds his strength. "Same as Ghalib's?" Alan says.

"Very same," Mohammad says.

"In the national strip?"

"Red with a white stripe," Mohammad says.

I sit with Alan in the clinic most days after school. He's pale and thin, but with bright eyes and a lively tongue that I never want to stop talking. He leans his head against my shoulder to ask endless questions.

Like "Why did you run away?"

And "Where did you find Safaa and Amin?"

And "Did you miss me?"

I answer as well as I can and promise to bring Amin and Safaa to visit as soon as he's well enough.

When Dayah, Baba and Bushra are with us, we all talk endlessly about what happened after I crossed over. We have so much to share.

"They closed the border completely, even to trucks and buses," Baba says. "People left. Walked back into Syria."

"But not us," Alan says.

"We stayed, sleeping outside night after night," Bushra says. She's lost weight. Dark circles under her eyes, sharp lines etching her cheekbones. This has been hard for her. For everyone.

"It was horrible," she says. "We had only chocolate and crackers from the sup-sup van. My back still hurts from sleeping on the ground."

"Baba found men to help us," Alan says.

"People smugglers?" I say.

"You know about them?" says Baba.

"Some boys here crossed over with smugglers. Got robbed by them too."

Dayah fingers her neck. Several gold necklaces are missing.

My breath catches. "Were you robbed?"

"Not robbed," Dayah says. "But it was so expensive."

I feel so bad for my family.

"Gold is nothing, Ghalib," Dayah says. "I would have given my soul to find you."

"They walked us for hours along the perimeter fence," Baba says. "Mostly at night when it was cooler and we wouldn't be seen. Away from the border, into the hills."

"With only hard biscuits and crackers to eat," Bushra says.

I remember my hunger, my endless thirst in the Turkish hills. I look at Alan.

"We're lucky you're here, Alan," I say to him. I hug him tight.

"Alhamdulillah," Dayah says.

"The smugglers carried water," Baba says. "They rationed it by day. Nothing at night."

"How did Dapir manage the hills?" I think of Dapir climbing, struggling, wheezing. Never complaining. I'll carry her loss in my heart forever.

"They were hard for her," Dayah says. "She ran out of energy, even when Baba carried her on his back."

"She went to sleep on our third night of walking," Bushra says. "She was tired, but she wasn't hurting. She didn't wake the next morning."

There's dark all through my blood.

"If I hadn't run to the border, Dapir might still be with us now," I say.

Baba shakes his head. "Leaving Syria was too much for her."

I want the story to be happy again. I want to feel bright through my blood again.

"Finally we arrived at a place where the perimeter fence was cut through," Baba says. "No searchlights deep in the hills. No one to see us."

"I was first to cross over," Bushra says. I smile. She smiles back.

"The smugglers left us then," Baba says. "We were on our own once we were in Turkey."

"How did you get here?"

"Bushra brought us," Baba says.

"Bushra?"

"She was so strong, so brave," Dayah says. "She was determined to find you."

A rush of surprise heats my face, and my heart fills with happiness.

Bushra turns away when I look at her. "I heard people talk of this camp," Bushra says. "I hoped you might have come here."

"She made me walk when I wanted to rest," Alan says.

"She kept our hopes of finding you alive," Baba says.

"Thank you, Bushra," I say.

She looks at me. She hears how much I mean it. "It was easier for me, Ghalib. I was with family. You did it on your own. That's real bravery."

This is the second time she's said this to me. Some small part of me begins to think that perhaps I'm not the coward I believe myself to be. Maybe I am a little bit brave after all.

Fatima moves me from the children's center into one of the shared tents in the Kurdish section with my family. I didn't know there was a Kurdish section. It's in the oldest part of the camp, where Safaa and I never walked, on the other side of Green River. The paths are gravel and the toilets don't overflow. There are Kurdish weavings and patterned rugs, and everyone speaks my language. The women in their beaded scarves and brightly patterned skirts are strong and equal to the men. Some people have even planted green herbs and flowering bulbs around the tents. It feels a little like home.

But the old tents aren't so comfortable to live in. Lots of people have to cram inside. We share with three families: fifteen people in one tent. Sixteen when the doctors send Alan home. Empty potato sacks and orange onion bags cover the dirt floor. We can never seem to get rid of the clouds of flies. Dishes and cups, plastic basins and sacks of clothes, packets of food, and water containers are stacked everywhere, with our blankets and cushions and rugs. Our tent smells of smoke and unwashed bodies and greasy food.

"The smell's coming from over there," a woman in our tent says. She nods toward the far end where a family of five has taken over half the tent, and wrinkles up her face to show how bad the smells are.

"They've been here a long time," she says. "Longer than anyone."

She says it softly as though afraid of waking a monster. We look at the woman. We say nothing. As well as taking up half the tent, the long-time family has extended outside their area with a makeshift shelter of plastic sheeting and bamboo.

"Are they allowed to do that?" I say.

"It's none of our business," Dayah says. "So we won't be saying anything."

"Just because they've been here forever, it doesn't give them the right to take over half the tent," Bushra says.

"Don't start, Bushra." Dayah's voice has that warning edge.

"They're hogging all the space," Bushra says. "Everyone should share equally."

"We've only just arrived," says Dayah. "We don't know their circumstances."

We hang blankets and woven rugs from the top pole to divide the remaining space, so each family has some privacy. Baba isn't that concerned about how the tent is split up. He's more anxious about not getting in touch with Uncle Yousef and the mukhtar.

"It's been longer than I said," he says. "They'll think something is wrong."

"A lot *is* wrong," Bushra says. "Dapir is dead. Alan is sick. Ghalib got lost."

"Hush, Bushra," Dayah says.

"I need to let them know we've made it to Turkey," Baba says. "And find out about Hamza."

"There's a signal behind the clinic," I say. "People can text and message there."

"My battery's dead." Baba peers at his phone. "And it's not even set up to use in Turkey."

"The phone man charges them with a car battery," I say. "He sets them up for Turkey and sells credit."

Baba and I join the line at the phone man's tent. He leans over the car battery on a fold-up table, adjusting clamps and cables and connections to six phones. Loud haggling and bargaining fill the air. When it's our turn, the phone man agrees to charge and set up the phone in return for water-purifying tablets from Baba's pharmacy back home. He pries the card from Baba's phone.

"Keep this to try for a signal from Syria," he says.

As soon as the phone is ready to use, Baba heads off behind the clinic. It's almost dark when he returns. He looks happier.

"Hamza is doing well," he says. "He's breathing on his own. They're happy with his progress."

It seems so long since Hamza and I ran down Aleppo Way to find shoes. And only now is he breathing on his own. It will be a long time before he and his parents follow us. "There have been more explosions, more airstrikes, but none near our home," Baba says.

"Did you tell them about Dapir?" says Bushra.

"They send their prayers and blessings for Dapir. And for us all."

Since I found my family, something has changed between Bushra and me. Before, she was difficult to talk to, always snapping at me, but now she's easier to be with. Instead of turning away from me, she smiles and talks to me like I'm a real person. It feels different. It feels nice. When Dayah sends us to collect water, Bushra and I talk about home and the camp and Dapir while we wait to fill our containers. Afterward we join Dayah at the kitchen burners. It's a long wait.

"They need twice as many burners," Dayah says. "It'll be dark soon."

Nobody wants to be left in the kitchen when it gets dark. The camp isn't a safe place after light seeps from the sky. There's no electricity to light the tracks and toilet huts and kitchens. Everything sinks into the night. It's easy to trip and break an ankle on uneven paths and broken stones. To get lost among endless tents and makeshift shelters as you try to find your way home. People even disappear. One girl never returned to her family after she went to the toilet. Her father heard her scream, but when he searched for her, all he found was her shoe. And two boys were kidnapped.

"Forced into ISIS," Bushra says.

"We don't know that," Dayah says.

"Kidnapped girls are married off," Bushra says. "Or trafficked to other countries."

"How can you be so certain?" Dayah says.

"Bushra knows these things," I say.

Bushra looks grim. "There are men who come out at night like the rats that swim in Green River."

Most people stay inside as the moon turns, only reappearing to break their fast when the sun rises and camp comes to life again. Dayah frets if we're still lined up waiting for the kitchen burners when the sun drops behind the distant hills.

"We need to get back," she says.

"Just another few minutes," I says.

"We're almost at the front of the line," Bushra says.

So far, we've always gotten back to the tent in time. Sometimes we hurry when twilight is already thick and soupy. We rush along the dirt tracks, hot food slopping, water sloshing. We close the flaps of our tent, settle safely in for the evening to eat our meal.

Even though things are good with Bushra, Safaa and I are awkward and uncomfortable somehow. She doesn't want to visit my family in the Kurdish section.

"We're not Kurdish," Safaa says. "We're Armenian Syrian."

"Doesn't matter," I say. "You know my family."

"It would feel strange for me to be in the Kurdish section."

"We don't bite. And you're only visiting, not moving in."

But she still won't come. I see her every day at school, but she doesn't want to talk so much now that Bushra is with me.

"Will we walk after school today?" I say.

"Maybe tomorrow."

"Can *I* walk with you, Ghalib?" Amin says.

"When Safaa comes, then you can come too."

Safaa takes his hand. "Ghalib needs to spend time with his family."

She turns away, leading him back to the children's center.

"After school tomorrow then?" I say.

But Safaa doesn't reply. I feel sad for them, especially Safaa. I think she's a little lost now that my family has come. It must be strange and lonely for her and Amin to be alone again, but it doesn't have to be like this.

The doctor finally discharges Alan after almost a week. He's a bit wobbly of foot, though no worse than he is most mornings. His new white trainers support his bad foot and help him walk straighter.

All he needs is a little exercise to loosen up his stiff leg. As promised, Mohammad gives him a red tracksuit that will probably still fit him when he's getting married. Alan is so proud of it and wants to show it off to everyone.

"Can we visit Safaa and Amin, Ghalib?" he says.

At the children's center, Alan and Amin are awkward and shy with each other, unsure what to say. I feel the same with Safaa. It's easier to focus on the two boys instead of talking with her. Amin jumps up and down with excitement. He strokes Alan's face and the front of his new tracksuit. Alan looks at Amin, smiling. He says nothing at first.

"You're doing well, Alan," Safaa says.

"He needs to fatten up to fill out his tracksuit," I say.

Alan acts like a baby, trying to climb into Safaa's arms as he's seen Amin do. Pretending to be younger than he is. He's playing it up. His weak arm is more hooked than ever.

"You'll never be good at soccer if you don't practice your skills," I say. "Straighten your arm and show Safaa how good you are."

He pulls a face and stretches out his hand. He and Amin run off to find a ball. Minutes later, they're playing an awkward game with a half-deflated soccer ball—Alan with his gimpy leg and crooked arm, Amin with two left feet and uncoordinated tackles.

"They'll never make the national team," I say.

Safaa's laughter shatters our awkwardness like glass breaking. From that moment, we're comfortable again, sitting on the broken-down fence. The disquiet of recent days burns away like morning mist.

17

"Not again," Bushra says.

It's dark. We're curled up in our blankets, almost asleep. I turn to where Baba and Dayah lie.

"I don't want to go again, Baba," I say.

Now we are all awake. Even Alan. Baba turns on his little battery flashlight so we can see him—this is an important conversation. His face glows ghostly white.

"Keep your voices down," he says.

He gestures toward the hanging blankets dividing the tent. Other families might be asleep, but I doubt it. They're probably wide awake listening to us. Hearing this big news at the same time we are.

"I like it here," Alan says. "Can't we stay, Dayah?"

"This is no place to grow up," Dayah says.

"I don't want to grow up," Alan says.

"We don't have to stay forever," I say. "Just a while."

"In a refugee camp?" Dayah says.

"What's wrong with that?"

"Where do you want me to start?" Dayah says. "There's no privacy. No proper toilets or kitchens. No facilities for a growing family."

"I have no work here," Baba says. "The sanitation is terrible—it's only a matter of time until one of us gets sick."

"I was sick already," Alan says.

"Bushra and I go to school here," I say. "Before I got here, I hadn't been to school for months." Education is always a strong argument to put forward. I'll never get to university on the education I'm getting here, but my parents don't need to know that right now.

"Why are we always leaving?" Alan says. "We left Kobani and Hamza. We left Syria and Dapir. Now we're leaving here. Who will we leave behind this time?"

He looks at us as though trying to decide who should be left behind.

"We only came here to find Ghalib and get you well again," Baba says. "We were always going to go farther than the first refugee camp."

"There are nice people here," Bushra says. "Kurdish people. I have friends again. Don't you want me to have friends?"

Bushra walks around the camp with girls from school, like I do with Safaa and Amin and Alan. She stopped laughing for a long time, but she laughs here, like she used to in Kobani.

"Bushra is right," I say. "She's happy here."

Bushra looks at me to check that I'm not teasing her. Seemingly satisfied, she turns back to Dayah. "Don't you want me to be happy?"

"There are no bombs. No airstrikes," I say. "No ISIS fighters."

Baba shakes his head at us. "This isn't a safe place at night."

"In Kobani it was dangerous day *and* night."

"We have to find a permanent home where we can settle and stay," Baba says.

Dayah looks at Bushra: "A home with new friends to make you happy." She looks at me: "Good schooling so you can go to university." She looks at Alan: "And where you don't have to leave again, even if you don't want to grow up."

Bushra scowls. "You worked this all out," she says.

Here we go, I think.

"You and Baba are ganging up on us about this." She looks at them closely, screwing up her eyes. "You planned this whole conversation. There's nothing Ghalib and I can say to make you change your minds."

"Or me," Alan says.

"Or Alan," Bushra says.

"What are you talking about, Bushra?" Baba says.

"You figured out every argument we could put up against leaving and worked out an answer before we even thought of the arguments," Bushra says.

She turns to me. "There's no point even trying, Ghalib. No matter what we say, they'll have an answer for it. Just go along with them. They'll win anyway. They're parents."

She emphasizes the last word—*parents*—as if it's the worst thing in the world. Bushra is being dramatic. My parents have to make decisions that are best for us. Leaving the refugee camp is probably the best decision, though it's a hard one.

"We didn't plan anything, Bushra," Dayah says. "We wanted to talk to you all about it."

I always knew we wouldn't stay here forever, but I didn't want to think about it. It's easier to not go anywhere. To write stories in school and walk with

Safaa and Amin and Alan. To line up for water and showers and burners and food rations. To shut ourselves inside overnight.

"I don't want to leave either, Bushra," I say. "I hate being on the road, but I don't want to grow up here. I still want to be a pharmacist. You still want to be an engineer. We'll never reach our dreams here."

"I left my dreams in Kobani," Bushra says.

"You have your whole life to weave new dreams," Baba says. "We're leaving for Europe."

"*Europe?*" Bushra says.

"Our final destination all along. It's mostly safe and peaceful, with work opportunities and good schools."

"What if Europe doesn't want us?" Bushra says. "It's closing its borders to people like us."

I stare at her. "How can a whole continent lock people out?"

"We'll claim refugee status in Europe," Baba says. "They have to protect us. To settle us with homes and jobs. You can go to school. Make friends. Stay in one place."

"Where did you hear all that?" Bushra says. "From the smugglers who wanted gold for fence clippers to cut into Turkey? It's not like that, Baba.

Europe is sending refugees back to where they came from. On planes and boats. Under armed guard."

Bushra is annoying me now, or maybe she's scaring me. I'm not sure which.

"Dayah and Baba are trying their best," I say. "All you can do is moan and make stupid comments. Why can't you be positive for once? Why can't you just get on with things?"

"Don't get upset, Ghalib," Baba says.

But it's not me who's upset. To my astonishment, Bushra's eyes fill with tears. They glitter in the wavering torchlight.

"Europeans don't know anything about Kurdish ways. They don't want us, Ghalib. Nobody wants us. They all speak different languages so we won't understand anyone and nobody will understand us. They'll stare at my headscarf and Kurdish clothes. They'll send us back to Syria, where we'll be bombed."

Bushra stops talking. In the breath-held silence that follows her outburst, she buries her face in her blanket. Her shoulders shake as she sobs. If the other families in the tent were asleep before, they're definitely wide awake now. They'll have plenty to talk about tomorrow.

I stare at my sister. "It's not my fault we're Kurd-ish," I say. "Don't blame me!"

"That's enough," Dayah says.

"Everyone's tired," Baba says. "We'll talk again in the morning."

That ends the conversation. Baba turns the lit-tle flashlight off and we lie down. In the darkness, Dayah murmurs soft words to Bushra, comforting her. Nobody comforts me. I can't see their faces and gestures, their fear and anger, but everything knots inside me. There's a hard ball in my belly. I lie in the dark and listen to my family breathing. I think they're like me, with aching hearts and racing thoughts. My head fills with thinking until it hurts. Maybe Bushra is right. Maybe nobody in Europe wants people who've had to run away from ISIS, from bombs and airstrikes. Maybe they believe we deserve to be blown up. Part of me is relieved to be leaving camp; most of me is terrified. I'm scared of my future. Where will I end up? What kind of life will I have?

And then there are Safaa and Amin. Baba never mentioned them coming with us. Now that we're friends again, they come around most days after school. They help prepare food and, some evenings, even share our meals. Surely we can't leave them behind?

Next morning, none of us talks about leaving camp. Everyone looks tired and red-eyed, Bushra most of all. I don't think she got much sleep. She walks to school ahead of Alan and me, her head down. I leave her to it. I don't want to listen to her scary talk and angry outbursts this morning. I don't want to talk to my family about leaving either, but it's entirely different with Safaa. During our afternoon walk, as soon as Amin and Alan run ahead to collect stones and twigs to build their own refugee camp, I burst out with the news: "We are leaving here for Europe."

"Families always leave," Safaa says.

"Will you come with us?" I say. "I haven't asked Baba, but he won't mind."

"We can only leave with our own family."

But Safaa has no family other than Amin. "What will happen, then?"

"We'll stay here," she says. "And you'll be gone."

Her words hold the same deep sadness and anger as her eyes, and perhaps even a little of their wildness. I don't want to leave them here. I especially don't want to leave *her* here. I want to say things—important things—but can't find the right words. I don't want them to come out wrong.

"If you were allowed . . . "

I stop. Try to think. Safaa waits.

"If you were allowed to leave camp . . . "

"Yes?"

"I would like you to be with me. I mean, with us. With my family." My cheeks are hot.

Safaa smiles. "I know."

She's like Bushra: she knows things before I know them. Maybe all girls are like this. Smart. Able to read a boy's thoughts before he even has them.

"You know?" I say.

"Of course," she says. "We're together every day. You're the closest thing to family we have."

I wait.

"If we were allowed to leave camp . . . " she says.

"Yes?"

"I would like to be with you."

She smiles. Her cheeks are pink. She looks away, pulling those dark eyes from me and taking my heart with them.

"Not only with your family, Ghalib," she says. "But especially with you."

18

Getting ready to leave Reyhanli Refugee Camp is nothing like getting ready to leave Kobani. We only have one corner of our shared tent to clear out. Dayah gives most of our belongings to the other family: extra blankets and cushions, cooking pots and water containers, old clothes and food. A few scraps belonging to Dapir. I think the other family is happy to see us go, and even happier to take what we leave behind. They're kind enough to give us their blessing.

"I hope they enjoy the extra space while they have it," Baba says. "It won't be long before a new family moves in."

Bushra looks at the bundle of goods I have ready to take. "You've changed since we left Kobani, Ghalib," she says.

"Two words, Bushra," I say. "Bare. Essentials."

I carry little this time. My bedroll, my blanket and towel, my zip-up wash-bag. My plastic bowl and woolly hat. Dayah gave me one of Dapir's scarves, which I wear with pride around my neck to remind me of her.

I wait until after school on my last day to speak with my teacher. "I'm pleased you're leaving," he says. "You're a caged bird here, Ghalib—this camp clipped your wings. You have much to offer the world. Go and fly."

On my last evening with Safaa and Amin, I give Amin my sports watch and soccer cards, and Safaa my treasured pocketknife.

"You don't have your gun," I say, "so this might come in useful. And maybe it can be something to remember me by."

"I would remember you even if you gave me nothing," Safaa says. She smiles at me from beneath her wild hair.

Dusk is closing around the camp as I walk them back to the children's center. I hug Amin tightly.

"Eat your vegetables," I say. "Get big and strong."

I turn to Safaa. I want to hug her too, but it wouldn't be respectful. We're uncomfortable and awkward.

"This is not the end," Safaa says. "Our futures will entwine, Ghalib."

"I hope so," I say. And I mean it.

I can do nothing about leaving Safaa and Amin, but I'm a little comforted by the certainty that I will see them again. Sometime, somewhere, our paths will cross.

We shake hands. Before I turn to leave, Safaa leans close to kiss me lightly and swiftly on the cheek, and then she's gone, pulling Amin with her into the children's center. It happens so quickly, I don't have time to react. I look after her. I touch my cheek with my fingertips as fireworks pop in my blood. I run back to our tent, through the thickening dark. The whole way, all I can think is: *Safaa kissed me!*

We leave the camp as early dawn pinks the sky in the east.

We turn our backs on the unwinding of a new day and walk west into the dark of the still starry sky. To Europe. A few early risers stop to watch us walk through the night-blue air. They stare because we are leaving. People who leave are always worth staring at. People who leave are the ones with hopes. With dreams. With choices. I've done my share of staring too: when the family I crossed the border with left a few weeks ago, I stared at them as they walked out the gate and I thought about the time I walked in with them.

Bushra doesn't like being stared at. "Do we have something stamped on our foreheads?"

"People who leave are the fortunate ones," Baba says.

"I don't feel fortunate," Bushra says.

"You have your freedom," Baba says.

"More than many people have," Dayah says.

"Nothing worse than moral lessons at dawn," Bushra says. She shifts her bag to the other shoulder and marches ahead.

I don't look back. I don't want to see the shelters and dirt paths, the makeshift lean-tos and Green River. I carry the smell of the camp on my skin and in my soul. It will always be with me. Now, I put my head down and lead Alan up the hill away from the entrance.

At the junction, a rusted signpost points to Reyhanli. I look at the painted plank of wood on the dirt bank, *Little Syria* spelled out in red paint. I remember standing here weeks ago with Musab and Ali, with the man and his family. I remember making the hardest decision in my life. I know now I made a strong decision. A brave decision. I made a better decision than I think Hamza might have made. I'm learning to keep my head about me.

We walk through the dawn, passing crops and meadows of wildflowers. Fields of wheat and cotton and grazing animals. They remind me of Syria before the war, when I went to the markets with Dayah and Dapir to buy lemons, eggplant, tomatoes. We cross a rushing river. Alan calls out to a startled herd of goats grazing along its banks. They skip and scamper, scattering for shelter among thick shrubs and hedgerows. Everything is green and fresh and growing. The sky has brightened by the time we arrive at the first buildings on the outskirts of Reyhanli: blocks of apartments and houses, mosques and schools and traffic. Alan's leg is stiff. This is the first time in weeks he has walked any distance. He clambers on my back. We walk alongside the busy roads until we reach the town center. It's waking up as we arrive in its morning-washed streets. A barber sweeps out his shop, stacks clean towels. The sign outside his door is in Arabic and Turkish. A baker washes down the path, sluicing water into the gutter. His trays are full of fresh baked goods: flatbreads, stuffed rolls, Syrian pastries. The aroma reminds me of home. I pause to read a café menu: traditional Syrian dishes among Turkish foods. I smell garlic, figs, sweet honey.

I don't understand the feelings gathering in my chest. "Why is it like this?" I say.

Baba looks at me. "What do you mean?"

I don't know how to explain the strangeness. Something is wrong about walking the streets of a busy market town so close to a refugee camp. We're so close to the Syrian border, which boils with guards and tear gas and people clamoring to cross. So close to hills where smugglers cut border fences to let people through. So close to where Dapir is buried in Syrian soil.

"It's so *normal* here." I don't know how to describe my feelings. "How is it possible? Our war is so close. People are *dying* just over those hills."

I watch children run past us on their way to school, backpacks heavy on their shoulders, clothes fresh, faces clean. Alan stares at them.

"Turkey doesn't have a war," Baba says. "The war is inside Syria."

I know this: Baba doesn't need to explain the politics of our war. But I also know he doesn't understand. My world tilts. The ground beneath me no longer feels the solid ground I walked on all my life. I look at a world I no longer understand. I'm grateful Alan is on my back to weigh me down or else I might float away.

"I know what you mean, Ghalib," Bushra says.

"Do you?" I search her face to see if she understands me.

She looks at the clean intact buildings. The well-dressed people. "Reyhanli is too clean for us. Too fresh. It's like we've stepped into a parallel universe."

Bushra *does* understand.

I think of what it's like in the refugee camp. I think of lining up for hours in the gathering dark to use burners in a makeshift kitchen, to fill water containers before night seeps through the path, before the camp sinks to a dangerous nothing until morning.

We put our bags down in a small square. Baba leaves to exchange gold jewelry for Turkish money and to find out information. Alan slides off my back. I stare around me. The strange feelings haven't eased.

"This is Kobani from five years ago," I say. "Before ISIS, before the bombs. Before the war."

"Lots of Syrians live here," Dayah says. "That's why it feels like home."

Dayah is like Baba. She doesn't see either.

"It's not that," I say.

"Why are the buildings standing up?" Alan says. Even he gets it.

We laugh. "Buildings are supposed to stand up," I say.

Dayah ruffles his hair. "You're too young to remember Kobani before the city was blown apart. You were born after the war started."

"I got born with the bombs," Alan says.

"You arrived at a dangerous time," Dayah says. The memory saddens her words.

"You couldn't get to hospital," Alan says. "There were too many explosions."

We all remember Alan's story. We all lived through it. The panic. The terror. We know how it ends. Alan doesn't remember, so telling it is his way of sharing his history with us.

"I was sick when I got born," he says. "I stopped breathing."

"You were very sick," Dayah says. "But Baba saved you."

"Except he couldn't fix my arm or leg."

"He tried so hard." Dayah says. Her voice is a whisper now. "And Bushra searched everywhere for a doctor."

Alan kicks out his bad leg, holds up his gimpy arm. "I got broken because of the war."

"That war has a lot to answer for, Alan," I say.

"Why can't we stay here?" Bushra says. "It would be easy to get home to Kobani from here."

She's right. Reyhanli certainly seems like a nice place. I look at the straight electricity poles with cables between them. Phone masts. Street lights. It's been so long since I've been anywhere with live electricity, with light and power after dark, I hardly remember what it's like to turn on a light switch.

"Too close to Syria," says Dayah. Her voice is soft. I think she's still remembering Alan's birth, which was also very nearly Alan's death.

19

We sit quietly until Baba returns, happy that he's managed to exchange gold jewelry for a thick wad of Turkish money.

"The bus terminal is on the north side of town," he says. "They call a bus an *otobus,* and the terminal is the *otogar.* We can get from there to Adana."

He hands us bottles of water and Syrian pastries, crunchy with pistachios and dripping with honey. We enjoy the rare treat in the little square in the middle of Reyhanli. Even though this place feels strange, I like how peaceful it is.

The *otogar* is a collection of little huts and low buildings on the side of two wide sets of train tracks.

With crowds of people, heavy traffic, uniformed officials shouting and directing, it reminds me sharply of the Syrian border. My belly clenches involuntarily, but once we get close, I see it's entirely different. As soon as we're within shouting distance, three or four bus hawkers immediately surround Baba, negotiating the best price to Adana. Baba speaks no Turkish but it doesn't matter—the hawkers switch instantly to Arabic. They try to talk each other down.

"Anywhere in Turkey! Anywhere in Turkey!"

"Today you leave, today you arrive!"

"No delay. Fast delivery of your family."

"Cheaper price with our otobus."

After a few minutes' confusion, Baba agrees a price and an otobus. Money and tickets exchange hands.

"We leave for Adana in half an hour," Baba says.

Half an hour in Turkey means the same as half an hour in Syria: the otobus doesn't leave until it's full. There are no assigned seats—everyone crams in wherever they find space. Alan and I are first onboard.

"Down the back, Ghalib," he says.

We jam ourselves in a little corner to watch the activity. Dayah and Baba sit up front. Bushra is in a little single seat. Once the bus is full, the bus attendant slams the sliding door and stands in the stepwell as we speed out of the otogar. Other passengers talk above the Turkish music blasting from the speakers.

I hear their conversations but understand nothing. Alan's head quickly gets heavy against my shoulder. Turkish countryside skims past, but I see little of it. I soon doze off, waking with a lurch when the driver beeps his horn.

We're pulling into a large modern otogar. The otobus is half empty. The bus attendant now sits up beside the driver.

"Where are we?" I say.

"Adana," Dayah says.

I nudge Alan awake, lean forward and poke Bushra. We clamber out, half stupid with sleep, and dump our bags on the ground.

Baba is all smiles. "Adana was closer than I thought. Who's hungry?"

"Me!" Alan says.

"What time is it?" I say.

"Time to eat," Baba says. He winks at me. I haven't seen him so lighthearted in months.

We take our bags and follow him through the doors of the massive otogar. It smells hot and foreign. There are shops and cafés, stalls selling mobile phones and shiny electronics. We pass a busy ticket hall full of vendors and rows of glass hatches, lines of seats and signposts. Hundreds of people mill around, running, trailing children and baggage, waiting in lines. All the signs are in Turkish—no Arabic here. We've left Syria far behind. Saying good-bye to Safaa and Amin in the refugee camp feels like it happened in another life. I struggle to remember Hamza's face.

"Stay together and don't get lost," Baba says.

I turn to take Alan's hand, but he's not beside me. With a rush of panic, I look back. He hops on his good leg across the shiny floor tiles.

"What are you doing?" I say.

"You can only walk on the black squares, Ghalib. You're not allowed on white squares."

He balances on a dark tile and hops to the next. I take his hand and we run to catch up with Baba, who waits for us at the door of a café. Dayah and Bushra are already inside. We load our bags against the wall and are about to sit down when someone shouts. A man rushes from behind the counter. He's wearing a greasy apron, waves a tea towel. He speaks in Turkish to Baba.

"I don't understand," Baba says to him.

The man raises his voice. He turns to me. I smell cigarette smoke from him. I don't know what we've done wrong but this man is not happy about it.

Other people in the café turn to look. They stare at us. Our bags. Dayah stands up and the man shouts at her too. Points at our bags. When we don't do what he wants, he leans down and grabs two of our bags. He points toward the door.

"Maybe we aren't allowed to bring our luggage inside," Bushra says.

"We can leave them outside," Dayah says.

Another man comes over, a customer in the café. He's young, with a beard, carrying a book and a backpack. "He says no Syrians allowed," the young man says to Baba in Arabic. "Are you Syrian?"

My blood freezes. I look at the young man. Baba looks at him, then nods. He says nothing. Nobody says anything, except the shouting man. The whole café has fallen silent. The whole café waits to see what will happen next.

Behind me, I hear Bushra mutter. Her voice skims above her breath. I'm the only one to hear. "Think this is bad? Wait till we get to Europe."

I want to punch her in the nose. I do nothing. I say nothing. I'm paralyzed.

The young man talks to the shouting man in Turkish.

The man shakes his head. Crosses his arms. Stands firm.

"He says Syrians are not welcome in Turkey," the young man says to Baba. "He says to leave his café. To go back to where you come from."

"Bushra, Ghalib, the bags," Dayah says.

We snap out of our stupor and grab the bags. Alan clings to me.

"Come on, Alan," I say.

He starts to cry. He's frightened. I don't look at anyone. My face is hot with shame. I drag the bags and Alan out the door. He stumbles over his feet because I hurry him. That makes him cry harder. Bushra is behind me. Her face is flaming. Her eyes are downcast. Then Dayah and Baba, with the young man.

"He says he put a sign on the door," the young man says. We look. A cardboard sign in Turkish and Arabic is stuck inside the door: *No Syrians.* The Arabic is not written properly but the message is clear.

The young man looks embarrassed. "This is not typical of Turkey," he says. "Not characteristic of my people. Syrians are welcome here. I'm sorry, but he wouldn't change his mind. He's angry about a lot of things."

His eyes are sad. He says more comforting things but I want him gone. I want to be a thousand miles away from this café. From this otogar. From Adana.

I want to be back in Reyhanli. Back in the refugee camp. Anywhere but standing outside this stupid café with its staring customers and badly written cardboard sign.

Alan is sobbing now. I pick him up. He nuzzles against my neck.

Baba nods at the young man. Thanks him for his help. "We'll find somewhere we're welcome," Baba says.

And finally we move away from the front of the café. We leave the young man staring after us.

Now that we've seen a *No Syrians* sign, we find them all over the place. On the phone stall. Outside the coffee shop.

"There's one," Alan says.

"There's another," Bushra says.

My insides curl up. I think of that man shouting. I blink hard to keep my tears back. People stare. They talk and whisper. I think it's because we're Syrian. Someone shouts and my heart skips a beat, but it turns out to have nothing to do with us. I keep close to Dayah and Baba.

"Let's get out of here," Baba says.

We leave the *otogar*. To cheer us up, Dayah buys slices of hot Turkish pizza and sweet sticky dough at a street stall. The seller teaches us Turkish as he hands over the food, wrapped in greaseproof paper.

"*Lah-ma-cun*," he says, pointing at the pizza. "*Lahmacun.*"

He leans over so Alan can reach the hot sweet dough with his good hand.

"*Sim-it*," the man says. "*Simit.*"

We sit and eat on a little patch of sunburned grass outside the station, well away from Turkish people. Baba has said little since we were thrown out of the café. His face has lost the happy look he wore when we first arrived. His words shrank to nothing in the face of the shouting man and he hasn't found them since.

After we've eaten and rested, though, we make a plan. "We need to get a bus to Izmir," Baba says. "Where the boats are."

"We're going on a boat?" I say.

"Across the sea?" Alan says.

Baba nods. "From Izmir to Europe."

I've never been on a boat. I've never seen the sea.

"Where in Europe?" says Bushra.

"Who cares?" I say. "It's not Adana."

"Greece," Baba says. "We'll get a boat from Izmir to the Greek islands. Greece accepts Syrians."

"Do they bomb on the Greek islands?" Alan says.

"No bombs."

"Do they shell on the Greek islands?" I say.

"No shells."

"Will they let us land on the Greek islands?" Bushra says.

— — —

The bus to Izmir is much bigger than the little otobus from Reyhanli. It has cloth seats and air conditioning and a separate place to store luggage. Dayah doesn't want to leave our luggage in the hold. "We can't see it. Somebody might take it."

"The driver locks the door," Baba says.

Dayah is not convinced. She puts the bedrolls and blankets in the hold; everything else comes onto the bus.

"Thirteen hours to Izmir," Baba says.

"How long is thirteen hours?" Alan says.

"More than one sleep," I say.

"On one bus?" He looks at me wide-eyed. "Won't we fall off the country?"

"Big country," I say.

Bushra and I share a seat in front of Dayah and

Baba. We raise the armrest and Alan sits in the middle. Alan and I check out the gadgets: ashtray, footrest, air vent, little net fixed to the back of the seat. "For your water bottle," I say.

Bushra is grumpy already. "Stay still!" she says. "Do you have to jump around so much?"

"It's going to be a long thirteen hours," I say.

A green light above the driver turns red. After a while, it goes green again as a man returns to his seat from the back of the bus. "There's a toilet at the back," I say.

"You're not investigating it now," Baba says.

An older couple gets on, arms full of bags. I know immediately that they're Syrian. This surprises me. I wondered how the shouting man in the otogar recognized us as Syrian but now that I see this couple, it's obvious that they look completely different from Turks.

Bushra looks at them too. "Is it their clothes?" she says. "Or their faces?"

Maybe it's their uncertainty as they scan the bus. "Do we look like that?"

"Maybe to others."

"They wear the war," Alan says. That's the best description of all.

The couple finds their seats. I'm pleased we're not the only Syrians on the bus.

We leave almost on time. The driver talks in Turkish over the speaker as I gaze out the window. Adana slides past, and I am not sorry to leave. I lay my head on the headrest and think about crossing the sea to Europe.

20

All through that afternoon and into the night we travel across Turkey. I half-wake each time we pull into a garage for fuel or stop to let passengers on or off. A breeze wafts through the open doors, the cabin lights with sudden brightness, I'm aware of shadows and voices. Most of the time, I sleep, slumped against Alan or Bushra.

I wake as the sky pales. Alan is now between Dayah and Baba. Bushra looks out the window. "See the sea?" she says.

We drive along high cliffs. Reaching from the cliff face to the far horizon is the bluest, flattest, sweetest sight I've ever seen. The ocean is still and calm, with a sparkle where the rising sun catches it. Even in its stillness, a roll heaves beneath its vast surface like a giant turning over in his sleep. Its farthest boundary is hazy. It melts into the morning sky. I've seen pictures of the sea. I've seen films and videos of the sea. But I've never *seen* the sea. And there it is, shining beneath me.

"I can't stop staring at it," Bushra says.

"We're going to cross it," I say.

The bus trundles for another hour before we reach the city of Izmir, where we disembark at the otogar. Baba pulls our luggage from the hold. "See?" he says to Dayah. "Nothing taken."

"Nothing worth taking," Dayah says.

The older Syrian couple we saw earlier approach Baba and Dayah. The rest of us wait with the bags while the adults talk quietly.

Dayah turns to us. "They will be joining us for a while," she says.

"Where are they from?" I say.

"Aleppo," says Baba. "They're traveling to their sons in Germany."

Izmir is a different city entirely from Adana and Reyhanli. It's buzzing and crowded, full of old buildings and open-air cafés, markets and green spaces. There are foreign people everywhere, and not only Syrians. People in skimpy clothes with sunburned skin and peeling noses. People with blond hair and orange hair and even one with purple hair. People in sunglasses.

"Europeans on holidays," Bushra says.

We see dark-skinned people with headscarves and long robes, women with their faces covered and children trailing behind them.

"Afghanis traveling to Europe," Bushra says.

"What makes you an expert on every nationality?" I say.

"I know these things. I read the Internet."

"That's what we need now," Baba says. He and Dayah want to get news from home, so we find an Internet café. The Syrian couple order Turkish coffee and eggs while we log on to a computer. Baba reads emails from the mukhtar, from Uncle Yousef, from others at home.

"How's Hamza?" I say,

"Alert and doing well. His burns are healing. He might be strong enough to travel in a few months."

"*Months?*" It seems like forever.

Dayah reads news from Kobani, after which Bushra checks her social media. She's on for ages.

"Hurry up," I say.

"There's a lot of news to read."

"I get time too."

When she finally gets off, I check the teams on the Syrian Premier League. The connection is too slow for gaming and none of my friends is online to chat. I wish there was Wi-Fi in the refugee camp so I could chat with Safaa and Amin. I want to tell them what the sea looks like and about our bus journey and the shouting man in Adana.

Once we're finished, we have eggs and bread. The older Syrian man introduces himself as Baraa and his wife as Rawan. She wears a lot of gold jewelry. They both have gray hair and are dressed in brightly colored clothes. They smoke a waterpipe. I stare at the water bubbling through the blue glass vase, the shining brass bowl with its wisp of smoke, the long hose wound around with copper wire. The smoke smells sweet and fruity. This couple might be senior citizens, but they're nothing like Dapir. My Dapir would never smoke a waterpipe in a million years.

"My sons tell us we must find the Sinbad Restaurant in Basmane Square," Baraa says. He looks around and drops his voice low. "Where Turks arrange for Syrians to cross to Greece."

"How much does it cost?" Baba says.

"More than most people have." Baraa says. He

rubs his belly. His wife turns gold rings on her fingers.

"There are only two of us," Baraa says. "Are you bringing all the children?" He looks at the three of us. He drops his voice, but we hear him anyway. "Would you not leave the girl?"

Bushra says nothing—which is hard for her—but I see her jaw clench. She turns away. Baraa's wandering eye stops at Alan. He looks at his little hooked hand. His gimpy leg. I stiffen. I know what he's about to say next. We've heard it many times before in Kobani.

"And what use will that one be?" Baraa says. "He'll bring a curse on your family. Perhaps on everyone in the boat."

Dayah sits upright. She draws breath. "All my children are precious. I don't favor one over the other. I would stay behind in a heartbeat to let them go if we didn't have money for all of us."

Baraa inclines his head to acknowledge my mother's words. He makes no further comment. Secretly, I'm pleased he didn't pick on me—I'll definitely be in the boat. But I'm annoyed for Bushra and Alan. Baraa's wife, Rawan, says nothing. She sucks on the waterpipe and watches us silently, her jewelry glinting in the sun.

Plastic tables and chairs are set on the pavement outside the Sinbad Restaurant. Crowds of people stand around. Some look Syrian. Others have darker skins, wear different clothing and speak unfamiliar languages. A lot of them message or talk on their phones.

Inside the restaurant, half a dozen Turkish men watch from a small table. They spot us arriving. They follow us with their eyes. They remind me of Syrian shopkeepers who chased me and Hamza from the burned-out stalls in the souq. Of Turkish border guards with raised guns and loud voices who eyed everyone up at the Bab al-Hawa Border Crossing. Of the shouting café owner in Adana. Something unpleasant is in the air around this place, like the electric charge before a thunderstorm.

"The owner's brother manages his business from here," Baraa says to Baba. "You and I need to talk with him."

"We'll wait here," Dayah says.

Rawan waits with us. She doesn't speak, but glances around with the same nervousness I first noticed on the bus. A tall teenager approaches Baba and Baraa when they enter the restaurant. The hair on the back of my neck prickles and my skin tightens as I watch them, even though it's bright daylight with plenty of people around. Their discussion doesn't take long.

"We must wait until sunset," Baraa says when he and Baba return.

"And then?" Dayah says.

"We don't know," Baba says. "They won't discuss anything."

"But you're sure this is the right place?"

"He wouldn't confirm anything," Baba says. "Blanked us completely and only offered to take a food order."

"The authorities must be watching," Baraa says.

I cast my gaze around the narrow streets, the tall buildings, the knots of people. No police or officials are around but, even so, a shadow crosses my heart. We have no papers, no permission to be in Turkey. We're illegal.

"What will we do, Baba?" I say.

"Wait until dark."

The sun is still high and a lot of day stretches ahead. We settle at one of the plastic tables with our bags. Nobody comes to take an order. After a while, the attention of our Turkish watchers moves on to someone else. We're no longer the new arrivals. We melt into the crowds. What seemed exciting and adventurous this morning now has a sinister edge to it. The thought of crossing a vast stretch of sea is terrifying, especially if it happens after dark. I had never considered it might happen at night, with so many foreigners from unknown countries.

"I don't want to go in the boat, Baba," I say.

"We have no choice, Ghalib."

Hamza's words from another time, another place, flash into my head: *There's always a choice, Ghalib.*

"But at night! Can't we choose a daytime crossing?"

"It's safer when we can't be seen."

And that's the choice, which is not a choice at all.

"How will we know where to go?"

"These people arrange this all the time. They know what to do."

There's little talk among us: everyone seems caught up in private thoughts. Sometimes I tune into foreign conversations. Sometimes I watch others around me. Alan wanders among the scattering of tables, watching people curiously and smiling if they notice him. Some ignore him; others have a friendly word. I watch their faces. I know what will happen every time. I wait for that instant when they become aware of his curling hand, his gimpy foot. I've seen people's expressions change so many times before. They stare at him. Sometimes they pull back a little. They look to see who he belongs to. Alan sees the change but I'm not sure he understands it. My heart aches for him. He circles back to our table every so often, as though for comfort. He nuzzles Dayah or butts against me. When he feels safe again, he resumes his wandering.

Mid-afternoon, Dayah orders chips and Turkish pizza. None of us seems to have much appetite. We pick at the food, push it around our plates. I watch the sunlight slide between the narrow buildings. Now that evening approaches, I wish time would slow down.

"I feel sick," Bushra says.

"Like you want to throw up?" I say.

"Like I'm facing the end."

"Don't say that, Bushra."

"Baba," she says. "Is there no other way?"

"This is how it has to be, Bushra."

Darkness creeps through the streets too soon. Twinkle lights come on in shops, strung around open doors and windows to spill color onto the street.

Waiters light candles on the tables outside their restaurants; bar owners turn on neon signs. Electric light is everywhere, so different from the darkness of Kobani and the refugee camp. I'm amazed by its brightness, its colors, its warmth. But it does nothing to lift the darkness in my blood.

Inside the Sinbad Restaurant, fluorescent tubes flicker on. Blue light glares into the night, throwing hard shadows around the crowds. People have been arriving all afternoon, sitting on the ground in the square. Now with the lights on, they shuffle closer, drawn like moths to the moonlight. Baba and Baraa join them. I feel the same sickness as Bushra.

--- --- ---

Baraa and his wife, Rawan, finish their business with the owner's brother first. Now it's our turn. The Turk wants to meet all of us.

"Why?" Bushra says.

"To see our sizes, our weights," Baba says. "For the boat." We're silent as we think about this.

"If we must, we must," Dayah says.

She ushers us into the Sinbad Restaurant. Turkish men move back to give us space. The Turk sits at a table covered with a red plastic tablecloth, a teapot in front of him. He's fat, with stains down the front of his shirt. He looks at us with greasy eyes.

"What do you need from us?" Dayah says. The Turk looks at Baba before he answers. "Weights," he says. "It's all about bodies."

Dayah looks sharply at him when he says that, but the Turk doesn't notice. Or if he does notice, he must not care. He asks our ages, writes figures in his grubby notebook with a short pencil.

"No food. No water. No bags," he says to Baba. It sounds like he repeats this a million times a day. "Only people. No space for anything else. You understand? Dump it all."

"No water?" Dayah says.

"No water! No water!" the Turk says, speaking into her face. "Why does everyone want water? It's only an hour, you understand? Lots of water in Greece for everyone. Short journey—no water."

Baba and Dayah stay to finish business while we go outside. The dark feels safer than the brightness inside the Sinbad Restaurant. Turkish men work their way through the crowds outside, sorting them into order, checking their reason for being here. Anyone passing might think this is a restaurant for foreigners, with a lot of waiters. Battery lights flicker green and yellow in little glass vases on the tables. Teenage boys serve dishes of food.

"We're staying in a guesthouse by the seafront," Baraa says to me. He ignores Bushra and Alan, in the same way he ignores his wife most of the time. "Your parents are spending all their money on you. I hope you're grateful to them for giving you this chance at a new life."

He stands up and walks into the dark. Rawan trots behind him, carrying their bags.

"I'm not surprised Baraa's sons moved to Germany," Bushra says. "If he was my father, I would move away too."

21

The Turk calls Baba on the third night.

It's late and the square is dark. Bars and shops are shuttered; the Sinbad Restaurant is closed. I'm lying with Alan, Bushra, and Dayah on the ground, wrapped in blankets. Baba has stayed up, waiting for the call.

My eyes fly open when the phone rings. Baba fumbles in his pocket to answer. I sit up. Hear the Turk's voice, even though the phone is pressed to Baba's ear. Baba repeats the instructions.

"End of the street," he says.

"Half an hour," he says.

"Delivery truck," he says.

The Turk hangs up. Baba's face is pale and ghostly under the streetlight, his eyes red and watery. He hasn't slept much since doing business with the Turk. He was afraid he would miss the call.

"This will change our lives forever," he said to us the first night.

"For better or worse," Bushra said.

Sometimes Dayah took the phone while Baba slept, but even then, it wasn't restful sleep. He lay down for minutes at a time, and started at every sound. He constantly checked the phone's battery, the signal, for missed calls. Now he peers at me.

"We leave tonight," he says. His voice is a whisper.

I swallow the sickness in my throat. My skin feels as though ants are crawling under it. My blood itches. I roll my blankets.

"Leave them," Baba says. "Nothing goes in the boat."

He wakes Dayah and Bushra. We let Alan sleep a little longer.

"Bring the blankets and bedrolls," Dayah says. "It might be cold on the truck."

We're quiet as we get ready. The square is full of people sleeping in the open after handing over all their gold and money to the Turk. All through the last two nights, other phones rang, other people around us got ready to depart. We listened to them leaving. We waited for our call. I wonder if they all got to Europe, if Greece allowed them to land on its shores. Now it's our turn. We're not alone. Ringtones cut through the darkness, breaking the sleep of a dozen other people in the square, people who will travel with us. They too gather their families and their belongings. Baraa and his wife, Rawan, have been in the guesthouse by the waterfront since the first night. Their sons in Germany sent them money for a bed.

"They're old," Dayah says. "They wouldn't manage to sleep on the ground."

"They could offer to help us," Bushra says. She hasn't liked Baraa since he suggested she be left behind. "They could bring us bread. Store our bags in their room."

"He's traditional and conservative in his views," Dayah says. "He knows no different."

"He knew to come to us looking for someone to travel with," Bushra says.

I think of Baraa answering his phone in his private guesthouse, only to end up with us in the same boat to Europe.

When we're ready to leave, Baba lifts Alan in his arms and we join the straggle of people walking to the end of the street to meet the delivery truck.

We hear the grinding engine long before it pulls around the corner. Canvas sides are stretched over a metal frame, like dozens we saw crossing the border between Turkey and Syria at Bab al-Hawa. Its headlights are off. Three Turks get out of the cab to open the rear doors; the driver stays behind the wheel.

"Why so many Turks?" Bushra says.

Everyone crowds close, but the Turks don't allow anyone near the truck. They push people away. Clear a space at the back. One Turk calls family names, the others count people getting on. Families with children. A group of four men. A young couple with a baby.

The Turk calls out our family name.

Baba and Dayah step forward, ushering us ahead of them. Bushra plucks at my shirt. I reach back and touch her fingertips. Alan peers at me over Baba's shoulder, eyes wide and frightened.

"Man, woman, three children," the Turk says. His Arabic is bad.

He counts us, pushes us toward another Turk who helps us climb the tailgate. Inside is black. I stumble over someone's feet.

"Here, Ghalib." Dayah reaches for me.

"Where's Bushra?" I can't see her in the dark.

"I'm here."

We hunker together, spreading bedrolls on the planks. Alan clambers off Baba to nestle against me. I watch the silhouettes of other travelers as they climb on and find their places. The back of the truck is full and yet the Turk still calls names. A baby cries.

"I hope it's a big boat," I say.

"I hope there's more than one boat," a voice says.

Baraa! My heart tightens. None of us says anything: I think everyone in my family recognizes his voice. Maybe there was a separate collection for people in guesthouses.

Bushra whispers in my ear so nobody can hear. "We're all equal in the boat."

When no one else will fit in, the Turks slam shut the tailgate and slide the bolt. Their cigarette smoke drifts through the air. The truck rocks as they climb into the cab, then the engine coughs into life. The driver slams it into gear and we roar into the dark.

"How far?" I whisper.

"Three and a half hours," Baba says.

Izmir is a different city at night. Loud music rocks the air as we pass late-night bars and nightclubs. Flashes of colored light gleam through gaps in the canvas to slide across our faces: young and old, dark and pale. Everyone's face lifts upward to the unexpected brightness, eyes wide. Voices and laughter, cigarette smoke and strange sweet smells I don't recognize wash through sudden bursts of music and electric light. Alan clings to me, tighter with every explosion of sound and life from outside.

"It's only parties," I say.

We soon leave the nightclubs and late-night parties behind. We drive on smooth concrete until the driver turns off the highway to lurch over dirt roads. The loud music and shouts of laughter are replaced with a sleepy silence, all the deeper in the truck. There's little talk. Sometimes a soft word, a reassuring comment, passes between families, but mostly we're inside our own heads, thinking of what lies ahead. Even Baraa has run out of things to say. Alan falls asleep on my lap. I lean against Dayah, but it's not easy to doze in the back of a pitching truck. It's not easy to sleep with sickness in my belly and blackness in my blood.

When the truck finally stops and the engine turns off, my ears throb with abrupt silence that rushes into my head. "Where are we?"

"Assos," Baba says. "I hope."

"I need to pee," Alan says.

"As soon as we get out," I say.

People gather themselves, break open unused voices after the long journey. The bolt slams back. The tailgate swings down. A bright fresh tang swims into the truck.

"What's that smell?" Alan says.

"Salt water," says Bushra.

I inhale deeply. The sea smell cools my heated blood.

We climb out, drowsy after sitting for so long. Alan stumbles until his feet find themselves. By the light of the moon, I bring him to a stand of small trees where we both relieve ourselves. Everyone is standing around when we get back. The baby cries again. I see her in her mother's arms.

The Turks carry large plastic sacks and thick sticks. The moonlight glints on long knives tucked into their belts. I nudge Bushra to show her.

"What are those for?" she says.

We trudge after the Turks along a narrow road. The ground is soft beneath my feet but it doesn't feel like dirt. It takes me a few minutes to realize it's sand. Beach sand. Tall slender grasses whisper and rasp as we turn off the road to push through them. They prickle my ankles above my trainers. Their sharp tips itch my arms. Dayah guides Baraa's wife, Rawan. Baraa walks next to Baba.

It's dark out, but not black like it was in the truck. The moon spills its cool light to make shadows darker than sin. It sparkles the sand with tiny glints. We climb a dune, and a black sheet of sea spreads before us, its ripples silver-bright in the moonlight. Waves fizz and melt into the black sand. "I can't see lights on the horizon," I say. "Where's Greece?"

"The Turk said we would see it from the shore," Bushra says. Her voice is tight.

We turn along the beach and round a small headland. Assos nestles in a circular bay, its streetlights glimmering. A dozen boats bob on the waters of a small harbor.

"Are we going in one of those?" I say.

Bushra punches me in the arm and hisses in my ear. "Don't make yourself out to be even more stupid than you are."

"I only asked!"

"Don't you two start," Dayah says.

I didn't know she was right behind us. Bushra and I shut up and stumble on, sliding and sinking in the soft sand. Dayah walks more slowly over the dunes with Rawan. The gap between us widens.

Bushra digs me in the ribs. "Those private boats belong to rich people and tourists."

"How was I supposed to know?"

"Our boat will be a leaking old tub."

We walk under trees at the back of the beach. Moonlight can't get through the leaves. Several people curse as they trip on roots and fallen branches. Without warning, Alan butts against me, pushing me aside.

"What are you doing?" I say.

"There's a man asleep," he says. "I didn't want to walk on him."

I glance back and see the silhouette of someone curled up against a tree trunk.

"There's another," Bushra says.

Lots of people are sleeping among the trees. Others hunker low on the ground, watching us. A bad feeling creeps through me.

"Who are they?" I say.

"Maybe other people trying to get to Greece," Bushra says.

The reek of wood smoke and human waste and bad food thickens the air. It lingers beneath the trees where the sea tang can't reach. I hold my breath. I know that stench too well.

"A settlement," I say.

We pass tents and tarpaulin shelters, lean-tos and cooking fires. People lie in sleeping bags, surrounded by car tires and orange life jackets, empty food packages, crumpled papers, water bottles and crushed cans. Like Reyhanli Refugee Camp, but dirtier and more disorganized. And the smell. Everywhere the smell.

"Like the Syrian border," Bushra says.

Baraa's voice carries through the dark. "I didn't pay to be brought to a shantytown. Where are we going?"

Nobody answers.

Men with dark skins and long beards squat around the fires, watching us. Their eyes shine white in the glow from the embers. Some have blankets draped over their shoulders. Some are smoking, the burning tips of cigarettes bright in the black. They stand up as we pass, hitching grubby jeans over narrow hips and muttering to each other. The bad feeling in me rises.

"Don't look, Ghalib," Baba says. "Keep close to me."

The four Turks with us have spread along the length of our group. They hold their sticks in their fists and march us on, heads down. I'm glad they're with us. The Turk leading the group picks up the pace. We clear the tents and cooking fires. I look back. Men from the camp collect at the fringes of the trees to watch our group.

"Will they follow us?" I say.

"I hope not," Bushra says.

I hurry on.

22

Once we're back on the beach again, the Turks relax
a little. We slow down. We're at a different part of
the shore. A stiff breeze comes off the sea to lift a
sting of fine sand. The strong salty ocean rushes at us
in pale broken rages. It paws the dark shore like an
animal about to charge. Its mood has changed from
the smooth silvery water where we got off the truck.
Waves sizzle into the sand to gather and rush again.
This is an angry, dangerous sea, whipped up by the
onshore wind.

We walk along the water's edge over stones
and shells and damp knotted seaweed. I sense the
strength of the sea. Its cold depths. Its restlessness. I
think of its strange creatures. Of its hunger for boats
and people, swallowing them whole so they're never
seen again. My belly tightens. I lean away from the

breeze, its saltiness gritty on my skin, clumping my hair.

Bushra holds her scarf in place with one hand, grips my jacket with the other. Alan clings to me, hand deep in mine. His little hooked arm is curled tight against his body like an extraordinary seashell, pale and fragile. He tries to twist his legs through mine to get closer and closer again. Some of the twisting is from his gimpy leg, which throws him off balance when we walk on an uneven surface, but most of it is Alan pressing himself against me when he could walk straighter if he tried.

"Stop, Alan," I say. "We'll both fall and then what would happen?"

I untangle him, make him walk beside me. But he still leans against me, away from the dark sea and the blackness, as though trying to imprint himself into me so that we become one.

The Turks stop. Waves slop and hiss at my feet. Rawan leans on Dayah's arm. Baraa, for all his bluster, looks old and anxious next to Baba. Everyone gathers close. We stare at the water.

A man turns on his phone light. He shines the beam through the windy dark to see the churning water.

"What are you doing?" A Turk grabs the phone.

"No lights!" says another Turk.

The phone goes black. "Sorry," the man says.

"Do you want us to be caught?" the first Turk says.

"Why do you think we are doing this at night?" the second Turk says.

"They definitely don't want any lights," Bushra says in my ear.

I can't laugh. My muscles are rigid. "I saw the boat," I say.

In the brief flash of brightness, it was on show until the phone light was quenched. I know now why the Turks want no lights. The boat is a wreck. Wet slippery sides. Repair patches all over it. It's hardly a proper boat at all—just an inflated dinghy—and certainly not big enough for all of us. Even when we're plunged into darkness again, the ghostly outline of the raft, its rope held in the fist of a Turk who stands knee-deep in seawater, burns into my memory.

"Did you see it?" I say to Bushra.

She didn't, but she hears the terror in my words.

The Turks tip their plastic sacks onto the sand: tire tubes and life jackets. They kick them apart. Straighten straps. Sort them out.

When a Turk calls out our family name, we cluster around. My shins tremble. Life jackets hang across the man's arm: one, two, three, four. Baba counts them.

"I paid for five," he says.

The Turk is already strapping Bushra into hers. He pulls the cords hard. Ties them at the side. Bushra grunts and huffs. This is really happening. Faster than I'm ready for.

"Where is the fifth?" Baba says.

The Turk jerks his head toward Alan. "Too small. Nothing fits."

I pull Alan against me.

"I paid for five," Baba says. "You saw him in the restaurant. You knew he would be coming."

"I got the smallest jacket," the Turk says.

"Where is it?" Baba says.

The Turk holds it up. "Still too big."

"You said nothing about him being too small," Baba says.

"Not my fault he's so skinny," the Turk says.

He pushes Bushra aside. I look at my sister, fat and uncomfortable as she now is, stuffed in the bright orange jacket. "I can't breathe," she says.

Laughter fizzes inside me. Terrified laughter.

"You took money for five people," Baba says. "I want five life jackets."

The Turk starts strapping Dayah into her jacket. He looks at Baba.

"You paid for five people in boat," he says. "You get five people in boat. This is not cruise. Take it or leave it."

"I want a life jacket for my son," Baba says. His voice is hard. Low. Edged. I've only heard Baba speak like this a few times. If I were that Turk, I would give Baba a fifth life jacket. But the Turk thinks otherwise. He stops strapping. He stares at Baba.

"Then give him *your* jacket," he says. "You want to go to Greece or not?"

Baba stops. We stand on the beach. There is the boat. There are the men to launch it. Across the dark water is Europe. We have no money. No food. No belongings. What else can Baba do?

"We need to go," Baba says. The hard edge to his voice is gone. There's only soft dead air in his words. Like loneliness. Like darkness. "But my son can't swim."

Alan whimpers. I realize I've tightened my grip on him like I'll never let go. I ease my hold and rub his back to comfort him.

The Turk grunts. Shrugs. He turns back to Dayah. Finishes strapping her in. He mutters under his breath: Turkish words I don't understand, but his feelings are clear. The Turk doesn't help Baba with his life jacket. He's still angry. But something unspoken passes between the two men when he tightens the cords at the side. Baba looks into the Turk's eyes.

"My youngest," Baba says. His voice is like dead leaves. "I ask you. Please understand."

The Turk grunts again. Shrugs. Baba nods. I don't understand this conversation. It has no start. No words. Only some silent understanding between two strangers.

The Turk snatches up the last life jacket. The one he said is the smallest. He turns to me. Alan won't let me go. I won't let him go either. I clamp myself to him.

"Alan," Baba says. He reaches over.

"Leave him," the Turk says.

Baba lets go in surprise. I stare at the Turk, his breath almost in mine as he straps on the life jacket.

"They go together," the Turk says. "Both small enough."

"I'll take Alan," Baba says. "It's too much for Ghalib."

"No," Alan and I say at the same time.

"We'll stay like this," I say.

And so Alan and I are strapped into the one life jacket. The cords are crossed over and back, binding us as one. Alan puts his good arm around me, his bad arm curled snug between us. I wrap both my arms around him. He peers up at me. "I'm with you, Ghalib." I hear the smile in his words.

The Turk checks our straps, slaps me on the back. "In the boat," he says.

He grabs Bushra and tosses her into the dinghy. She tumbles onto the slippery floor and instantly vanishes from sight.

"You," the Turk says to Dayah.

She looks at him. Looks at Baba. She hesitates. I can't see her expression in the dark but I feel her fear. I have the same fear in my belly.

"Go!" says the Turk.

Behind us, other people are ready to board. Strapped in their life jackets or holding inner tubes, some with nothing, they shuffle close, urging us on. We're the first.

Dayah wades into the sea until she's knee deep in swirling black water. The man helps her into the boat with Bushra. The Turk grabs Alan and me by our life jacket. With a sickening swing, he dumps us into the boat. We slither along the floor, splashing and spluttering in a shock of cold seawater. We struggle to stand as the boat rises and falls with a terrible rhythm. We grab Bushra and Dayah. We cling together. Baba arrives next and we're all here—all five.

The boat fills quickly—ten, twenty people—yet still the Turks push more in. The woman with her baby. A family. Four men. Baba and Dayah pull us close. I grip a length of rope tied to the side of the boat. The seawater collects in a pool on the dipped floor. I fight not to slide toward it. My feet slither on wet rubber. My new trainers are soaked through.

The boat is so full, it no longer rises and falls with the waves. Instead, we wallow deep and heavy.

A voice rises above the wind and waves. It's Baraa.

"Where's the other boat?" he says.

He stands on the shore with his wife, strapped tightly in their life jackets. The Turks ignore him.

"I said where is the other boat?" Baraa says again.

"One boat," the Turk says. "Everyone together. Get in."

"I paid extra!" Baraa says angrily. "For my wife and me." His wife stands next to him. She says nothing.

"Everyone in one boat," the Turk says.

"He's right," says another man still on shore. "Too many people for one boat."

A few people with him mutter their agreement.

"We won't all fit," the man says. He stands firm with his family.

"One boat!" The Turk's voice is louder now. "Get in!"

People hesitate. The Turk lifts his stick. Other Turks move next to him and raise their sticks. Two people splash through the sea and into the boat.

"Start the engine," the leader of the Turks says.

The Turk holding the rope clambers into the boat. He brings a wash of sea water with him.

"You want in the boat or not?" the Turk onshore says to the people left behind. "No refund if you stay. Your choice."

"I paid extra for a boat without that cursed boy!" Baraa says. "We'll drown with him!"

A sudden silence falls, even among the Turks. Nobody says anything. My heart shrivels when I realize which boy Baraa is talking about. I squeeze Alan against me to protect him from the cruel words.

"Evil old goat," Bushra says under her breath.

The man with his family looks at Baraa. He spits on the sand in front of him, then clambers on board with his family. Now only Baraa and his wife are on the beach with the Turks.

The Turk in the boat lowers the motor into the water. He points to the controls. "Speed, direction, on, off. All from here." His accent is thick.

A mighty roar from the shore splits the night as a dozen men burst from the darkness. Waving life jackets and car tires and thick branches, they charge down the sand to attack us. A woman onboard screams.

"Men from the settlement!" Baba says.

Everything happens at once. Baba thrusts us into the bottom of the boat. The Turks bellow and lunge toward the men. Moonlight glints on long knives in their hands.

Baraa turns to see, and his wife plunges into the sea. She lunges for the boat. The motor coughs and splutters. Two men onboard reach out to grab Rawan. Baraa pushes the settlement men as they pitch into the sea. They shove him to the sand. They splash and wade toward us. Rawan slithers into the boat. She coughs and splutters as settlement men grab the boat to clamber on.

Men in the boat snatch up paddles to beat them back. Paddles strike heads, backs, arms, with horrible crunching, battering sounds. The boat tips. Cold seawater rushes in. Everyone screams.

With a sudden belch of smoke and a fountain of white water, the engine kicks. The Turk in the boat leaps into the water and wades ashore. The boat lurches and spins. Two from our group tumble into the waves and are lost. Baba digs his fingers into my shoulder to hold me safe. People shout and grunt and scream. Water splashes and churns. Most of the settlement men let go. They sink into the sea. The boat rocks and steadies. A man grabs the controls. We gather speed and buzz from the shore into deeper water.

Back on the beach, Baraa is on his feet. He wades out, but we're already too far. He shouts words we don't hear. He's too late. His wife stares at him. She says nothing.

One settlement man still clings to a rope trailing in the water. He's being pulled behind us in the sea. He gurgles and splutters in the water. The men in the boat pry his clutching fingers off the rope. He screams as he drifts off to sink beneath the black waves.

I stare at the water where I last saw him. My heart pounds. My hands grip the rope and the wet rubber. Alan howls.

Heads bob in the water. Small figures move onto the sand. Baraa stands alone. Then everything melts into the darkness as Turkey vanishes from sight.

23

We're the only humans in a dark and salty world. We pitch and dip on a heaving sea. We cling to each other and the slippery rubber.

I never thought a sea held so much movement. I never thought a sea held so much fear. All I can think of are the bones of drowned refugees, of our brothers and sisters who went before us, lifting and turning on the seabed below, drifting like bleached ghosts pulled by moon and tide. Fish and octopus and coral make watery homes in their empty eye sockets and tooth cavities. Up above them, our little boat rolls and plunges.

"We're all going to drown!" Bushra says.

"Shut up," I say. Her words make me more frightened than I already am.

Black waves loom over us and roll beneath us,

dark and shining. We lurch between cloud and water. Every wash over the side adds more to the water sloshing in the boat. Men with seawater streaming from their hair scoop up handfuls to toss over the side, but their efforts make no difference: the water still rises. It's past my ankles now. The man steering the boat fights to keep the engine in the water.

"Turn into the waves," one man says.

"Keep sidelong to the wind," another man says.

"Head straight across the water," a woman says.

But nobody knows for certain. Nobody knows anything about steering boats across open sea in the middle of the night. The engine splutters and coughs and whines.

"It won't hold up," a man says.

Men grab paddles and sweep them through the water. It changes nothing. The Turk said we would see the lights of Greece as soon as we rounded the headland. We've been plunging and rising a long time. There are no lights. I don't know if we've rounded the headland. I see nothing of land or sea. The water, the sky, the air are all made of the one blackness. It seeps into my heart and crawls through my blood. Only this dark, wet hell exists now. Wind whips my damp skin and hair, chilling me even though the air isn't cold.

Apart from people shouting instructions to the engine man, nobody talks. We're too busy clinging on, willing Greece to appear. But we aren't silent either. Noise fills our boat, and none of it is a comfort. People moan and cry out and vomit. They shriek when we dip beneath a trundling wave, gasp when we crest its top. They send salty prayers up to Allah or the contents of their heaving bellies down to the fish. Alan has thrown up twice already. Because he's strapped to me, everything he throws up is down the front of our life jacket. We're wet through from waves washing over the side. His whole body shivers.

"Are we going to drown?" I say to Baba.

"Stay strong, Ghalib."

Baba was never one to sugar lemons. We can only hold on and wait.

"Lights!" someone says.

I strain to see in the dark, but there is only black. We heave over a wave. There! A sprinkle of lights strung along a distant shore. We roll into the next trough and the lights vanish behind a wall of seawater.

"Did you see them, Bushra?" I say.

"Alhamdulillah!" Bushra says.

The sight of land gives everyone hope. Brightness wells inside me. This will end. With a direction to aim for, the engine man hunkers down and grips the controls, motoring our little dinghy through choppy water. Even though I only see lights when we crest a dark wave, it gives me something to live for. Maybe we'll get through after all.

"Greece, Baba?" I say.

"Looks like it," Baba says. He grips Dayah's hand.

"Look, Alan," I say. "Greece."

But Alan doesn't look. He slumps low, head sagging. He is heavy against me.

"Alan?" Baba says. He leans over and lifts Alan's chin. Alan's eyelids flutter. His skin is white, his lips blue.

"Cold, Baba," Alan says. His teeth rattle.

We have nothing to wrap around him. No blankets, no bedrolls. We left everything in the back of the truck. Our clothes are sodden.

"Not far now, son," Baba says. "We'll get you warm and dry as soon as we arrive."

The night isn't so black any more. Stars glitter in the western darkness, but the sky pales to gray in the east. Dawn is coming. Soon we'll see where we've come from and where we're going. The waves still break with foaming tops, the wind still chills damp skin, but with every rolling wave, I see the distant shore. Greece swells to a dark shape on the horizon. Its lights draw us in. I see the shape of the hills. Soon I'll see trees and houses. Then cars and people.

The engine sputters and dies.

Everyone falls silent. After such bright hope, my heart sinks.

"Water in the engine," a man says.

Our eyes lock on the engine man. He pulls the starter cord. The engine whines and dies. He pulls again. Harder this time. The engine whines and dies.

"The choke," a woman says. "Try the choke."

With the choke out, the engine whines, gives a little cough and dies. Whines, coughs and dies. It burps a puff of black smoke. Nothing more. Someone curses.

"Empty tank," a man says.

"Not even enough fuel to cross," a woman says.

More cursing, this time directed at the Turks. The engine man sinks to the floor like a deflated balloon. I stare at him as fear rises in me. He releases the rudder, slumps against the sagging sides.

"Keep steering! Keep steering!" a woman says. "We'll drift with the currents otherwise."

The engine man leaps up. "I know nothing about these things," he says. He grabs the rudder. "I sold shoes in Damascus."

With no power, we drift with the mood of the breeze and the pull of the tide. Seawater slops and slaps over the side. The men with paddles dip them in the water and pull hard. Greece gets no closer.

"It's teasing us," Bushra says. "Near but still too far."

The sky blushes from gray to pink to blue. The sun peeks above the horizon. Alan lifts his head to squint in the new day. "Are we nearly there, Ghalib?"

"I hope so," I say. "The sun will warm you."

With the rising sun, the waves calm. The wind stills. Sudsy foam no longer flies from the tops of waves, which are now only sharp little peaks. We have no power, but there are no scary waves either. I dare to release the rope I've gripped since we left Turkey. I straighten stiff fingers. My knuckles are chapped, battered raw by salt water.

"Look! Look!" a boy says. He points across the sea. For a second, I think we're near Greece. I spin to see as something dark leaps out of the water. It plunges beneath waves and vanishes from sight.

"What was that?" I pull back with fear.

People scream. The boat rocks as they leap away from the side. I grab the rope again. Wind it through my fingers. Another something leaps from the water.

"What are they?" I say.

"Dolphins," a woman says.

"They won't hurt," Baba says. "They're curious."

The dolphins jump around us for a while. Everyone relaxes, settles into the boat. We watch. They help us forget we're drifting on the open sea. I let go of the rope. Move my feet. Water splashes around my knees. Our boat is lower in the water. Every wave sloshes over the sagging sides, bringing more water. I nudge Bushra to show her. She questions with her eyes, but I'm afraid to say anything. Putting words to it will make it real. But someone else soon notices.

"We're sinking, we're sinking," a woman says. Her voice rises and breaks like the waves. She grabs her husband.

"We've been sinking since we left Turkey," he says.

My stomach lurches.

Bushra gasps and spins to me. "You knew?"

"I just noticed now."

"It wasn't so bad at night with the engine running," the man says. He looks at the water in the boat. "Now it's bad."

Panic spreads. People try to move from the floodwater but they have nowhere to go. The raft sags. We peer out at the dark shape of Greece.

"Too far to swim," a woman says.

"We'll drift until we sink," a man says.

"We will drown," a teenage boy says.

A family speaking another language talk among themselves. They point at the water, at the boat, at Greece.

"A boat! A boat!" someone says.

The buzz of a motor from another boat dances across the water. I stare at the other dinghy, jammed with people in every available space. Heads turn on it. People wave, but it doesn't slow down or change direction.

"They aren't coming over," Bushra says.

"They might not make it if they do," Dayah says.

The other boat slows. I hold my breath. It drifts for a while. It swings slowly around. The buzz of the motor changes as it heads for us. A cheer goes up on our boat. A couple hundred feet away, its cuts its engine. It drifts closer. The men and women on board, the children and old people, are much like us. They watch from their crowded dinghy.

"No room," a man says. "We'll get help."

"We're sinking," a man on our boat says. "Please tow us."

They think about this. There's talk, argument. At last the man shouts: "Throw a line."

We cheer again. It takes time for us to paddle our boat around. The waves keep turning us. The men work the paddles hard. Our engine man throws our rope again and again. Finally a woman in the other boat grabs it. She ties it to a loop on their boat. In comparison to theirs, our raft wallows dangerously low, its inflated sides loose and sagging. My blood starts to darken but I don't let it take over. I remind myself I am brave and strong.

The other boat fires up its engine. The rope snaps taut. A rush of seawater gurgles over us. Foam sprays high. We move through the water, slowly at first, then faster as the front boat gathers speed. We buzz steadily across the waves. I grip Alan and the slippery sides of our leaking craft.

Greece grows bigger. Hills fill with definition and depth. Trees and houses appear, scattered on the slopes, clustered into villages and towns.

"I see a beach," Bushra says.

"I see a car," I say. Sunshine glints on its windows. "Look, Alan!"

Alan says nothing, but he lifts his head. I can't take my eyes off the shore. Sweeping waves curl and break on a stony beach. Tiny figures stand watching us.

"Are they waiting for us?" I say.

"Looks like it," Baba says.

"Will they turn us away?" Bushra says.

"No, Bushra."

We're still a good distance from shore when the tow boat releases our rope. It heads straight for the beach, where people run to help it land. With no power, we drift in its wake until onshore waves catch us. They curve fast and strong, driving us toward the shore. They crash onto rumbling stones with a noise like thunder. They drag us in.

They drag us *down*.

It happens so suddenly there's nothing I can do. White churning water swamps our struggling raft. It flounders. In the final stretch, when land is within reach and people are running toward us, our dinghy flips over entirely. Every one of us is tossed into the pounding waves.

Alan and I plunge into deep water. We sink

beneath the surface, gasping and gurgling. Darkness flashes through my blood. Alan kicks and struggles. Salt water fills my mouth and nose. Churning ocean and muffled shouts fill my ears. I toss among rolling waves. I lash out and flail. I don't know what way is up.

I'm drowning.

My life jacket drags us to the surface. We pop above the waves. I choke and splutter. Cough salt-water. Suck in a lungful of air.

Another wave breaks over us. It hurls me to the floor of the sea.

Rolling stones grate my face, scouring off skin. Pain sears through me. I open my mouth to scream. Seawater rushes in.

My life jacket drives me upward again. I gasp for air. Blow bubbles. Two people stand firm in the water next to me. One grabs my life jacket. He hauls me from the suck of the waves. I'm in his arms.

Alan is not strapped to me. The sea has torn him away.

"Alan!" I scream.

I twist to look at the sea, the scattering of people struggling out of the water, the wreck of our little dinghy. Where is he? *Where is he?*

The man holding me unstraps my life jacket. He wraps a crinkly silver blanket around me. He speaks foreign words. He carries me toward the shore. I struggle to free myself, to find my brother, but my muscles won't work properly. I'm helpless. I choke and struggle for air. I can't breathe.

"Alan." The name gurgles in my throat.

Sickness rises in me. I throw up seawater. I cough. Splutter. Hang limp in the man's arms.

We're out of the water. People from the two boats are all along the shore, wrapped in silver blankets, sitting on the beach. Some lie unmoving, facedown in the sand.

"Ghalib!" Baba says.

I almost leap out of the man's arms. He carries me to Baba, Dayah, and Bushra. Pale and trembling, they too are wrapped in silver, their lips blue with cold. The man sets me on the stony beach. My legs collapse beneath me. My body is sick through and through. I have no strength. Baba holds me. He buries his head in my shoulder. He sobs, great heaving sobs that shake his body. We cry together.

"Alhamdulillah!" Baba says. "My son. My son."

"Alan?" I say. What happened to him?

Men and women from the shore wade into the sea. They carry out babies and children. They help people to fight out of the waves. Rawan flounders ashore, leaning on a man's arm. The woman with the baby drops to the stones to give thanks for their safe passage. But the crashing water can't drown the cries and screams of those who've lost loved ones.

A man stumbles out of the sea carrying a small boy wearing the Syrian team strip and no life jacket.

"Alan!" I say.

The man carries him to where we crouch. Lays him on a towel, cradles his head. Alan's pale arm curls across his chest. Baba lurches to him. They pull off Alan's tracksuit. Lift his shirt. Pump his chest. One. Two. Three. Massage his legs and arms. Breathe into his mouth.

He's white as candlewax. Stiff as bodies back in Kobani. More men and women run to where he lies. They have oxygen. Warm blankets. Silver foil. They do everything they can. They work so hard.

"Alan," Dayah says. "Alan." Her words are only a whisper. They cradle a lifetime of pain.

Bushra's arms are around me. She holds me tight. I can't breathe. I can't *breathe*.

I push Bushra off me. Pull myself to my knees, muscles numb and inert. I edge across the stones. Thrust through the people who've gathered around my brother. Men and women sense me near. They pull back. Let me through.

I kneel at his head, bending low so my face is against his cold skin. So my breath becomes his breath. I breathe into him. I breathe for him. I breathe with him. I breathe *with* him.

Alan lurches. Coughs. Throws up. His gimpy leg spasms and stiffens. His back arches, lifting his small body off the towel. I pull back. I wait. I watch. He gasps. He breathes. He *breathes*. When he relaxes his spine and sinks to the stones again, the people around me swoop in. Rubbing, warming, bringing life back to his white limbs.

Behind me, I hear the joy burst through Bushra's words.

"He's alive, Ghalib!" she says. "And we've arrived in Greece."

I lean back on my heels. I smile.

I am Ghalib. I am invincible.

WHAT MIGHT HAPPEN TO GHALIB NEXT?

Like thousands of refugees arriving from Syria to the shores of Greece, Ghalib and his family must now find somewhere safe to make a new life. He is fortunate that his parents and siblings are with him—many Syrian children are separated from their families as they flee their homes. Amnesty International's research shows that children are the most vulnerable refugees, facing violence, exploitation and sexual harassment. Human traffickers prey on children traveling alone, and many of them are known to have vanished.

Even with his family, Ghalib faces an uncertain future. Most refugees who arrive by boat are exhausted and traumatized by their ordeal; many are also ill or injured. By now they have no money and few belongings.

Families like Ghalib's often end up in a refugee camp or even a detention center on mainland Greece. These places are unable to provide for the long-term needs of so many distressed adults and frightened children. Some camps and centers have no running water, electricity or medical aid.

Other refugees end up homeless, living on the streets of Greek cities or hiding out in the mountains and forests of northern Greece and Macedonia, as they try to travel farther into Europe in search of somewhere safe to live. These refugees have no access to medical care, education, work, proper food or secure housing. Smugglers exploit refugees by charging exorbitant fees to smuggle them across European borders, hiding them in trucks and containers, where they are at high risk of abuse, injury, sickness, detection, and even death. They are often turned back at borders.

More and more countries are closing their borders to refugees coming from Syria. In 2016, Turkey made a deal with the European Union to take back Syrian refugees in exchange for Syrians living in Turkey who qualify for asylum in Europe. This controversial agreement is being challenged by human rights organizations because it may result in people being deported to the country they've just fled. Syrian refugees like Ghalib and his family could be sent back to Turkey or even to Syria.

Ghalib's father may be able to apply for asylum status for himself and his family in Greece (or in another country) but the application process is long and tedious, taking months, and often years. During this time, the family will be housed in a detention center, unable to work and with limited access to education, health care and decent living conditions. Those who are fortunate enough to secure asylum status receive humanitarian aid and assistance with establishing a new life in Europe. Only a small number of refugees are successful with their applications.

GLOSSARY

Alhamdulillah: praise be to God; Arabic term

Allah yusallmak: a typical Arabic reply to almost anything pleasant; it can be a response to someone saying "thank you" or "thank God for your safe arrival" or "good-bye"

As-salamu alaykum: peace be with you; Arabic term

baba: dad in Kurdish and Arabic

caravanserai: an inn with a central courtyard for travelers in the desert regions of Asia or North Africa

dapir: grandma in Kurdish

dayah: mom in Kurdish

ISIS: Islamic State of Iraq and Syria, a jihadist militant group that follows a fundamentalist Islamic doctrine

keffiyeh: a square of cloth, often embroidered, traditionally worn as a headdress (mostly by men) in Middle Eastern countries; Arabic term

Kurd: a member of an ethnic minority living in parts of Iran, Iraq, Turkey, and Syria.

Kurdish People's Protection Units: the main armed service of the self-proclaimed governing body of Syrian Kurdistan. The Protection Units, which include the all-female Women's Protection Unit, are mainly Kurdish, but they also recruit Arabs, Turks, and westerners.

ma'a as–salaama: good-bye; Arabic term

mukhtar: the head of a village or neighborhood in many Middle Eastern countries, usually elected; Arabic term

souq: a marketplace; Arabic term

CHILDREN OF SYRIA

Every character in this book shares a name with a real Syrian child who died as a direct result of the war in Syria. Here are the real children.

Ali Qutayba Al Rawi was a five-year-old boy who died when International Coalition missiles were fired on the city of Al Boukamal on May 16, 2016. His brother Musab Qutayba Al Rawi also died.

Amin Deyaa Al Jaber was a ten-year-old boy who died when government helicopters dropped barrel bombs on the town of Kafrouma on May 27, 2016.

Alan Shenu was a three-year-old Kurdish boy whose image made global headlines after he drowned on September 2, 2015 in the Mediterranean Sea while trying to cross to Greece with his family. His brother Ghalib Shenu also drowned.

Baraa Rateb Al Sa'aour was a ten-year-old boy who died when Syrian government forces fired artillery missiles in the city of Damascus on January 26, 2016.

Bushra Rahal was a seven-year-old girl who died when Syrian government warplanes fired missiles on the city of Aleppo on April 11, 2016.

Dima Alabbasi was a fifteen-year-old girl who, along with her parents and five siblings, was subjected to enforced disappearance by the Syrian authorities. They were arrested in March 2013 and have not been seen since.

Fatima Baha Al Din was a three-year-old girl who died when Syrian government warplanes shelled the city of Raqqa on May 11, 2016.

Gardina Zamzam was a girl who died when Syrian government warplanes fired missiles on Aleppo on June 18, 2016.

Ghalib Shenu was a five-year-old Kurdish boy who drowned on September 2, 2015 in the Mediterranean Sea while trying to cross to Greece with his family. His brother Alan Shenu also drowned.

Hamza Ali Al-Khateeb was a thirteen-year-old boy who was detained during a protest in Daraa on April 29, 2011, during the civil uprising phase of the Syrian civil war. He died while in the custody of the Syrian government.

Mahmoud Al Jalleli was a four-year-old boy who died from locally made rocket shells fired from artillery located in the city of Aleppo, May 16, 2016.

Mohammad Yahya Ziqiyeh was an eight-year-old boy who was shot by a government forces sniper in Aleppo on May 27, 2016.

Musab Qutayba Al Rawi was a seven-year-old boy who died when International Coalition missiles were fired on the city of Al Boukamal on May 16, 2016. His brother Ali Qutayba Al Rawi also died.

Najah Alabassi was a thirteen-year-old girl who, along with her parents and five siblings, including her sister Dima Alabbasi, was subjected to enforced disappearance by the Syrian authorities. They were arrested in March 2013 and have not been seen since.

Safaa Abdul Rahman Emo was a twelve-year-old girl who died when Syrian government warplanes fired missiles on Aleppo on April 23, 2016.

Yousef Issam was a seventeen-year-old boy who was subjected to enforced disappearance by the Syrian authorities. He was arrested in the town of Idlib in 2014 and has not been seen since.

ACKNOWLEDGMENTS

I would like to extend my warmest thanks to the following people:

Siobhán Parkinson and Gráinne Clear of Little Island Books, for giving me the opportunity to write Ghalib's story in the first place, and for their insight, skilled editing, and hard work

Conor Hackett, for his ongoing enthusiasm and advice

The refugees I met and spoke with in the Jungle Camp in Calais, who live in terrible conditions with great dignity, pride, and resourcefulness

Raneem Eprahim, for describing in wonderful detail what life was like in prewar Syria, and Suzi Button, for introducing me to Raneem

Sandra Cullen, for her valuable input, support and friendship

DISCUSSION GUIDE

1. The civil war in Syria is a multifaceted conflict involving government forces and rival rebel groups (including ISIS). ISIS laid siege to the northern Syrian city of Kobani in September 2014. The Kurdish People's Protection Units, a military group that consists mostly of Kurds, recaptured the city in early 2015 but continued to clash with ISIS fighters. During this time, US-led airstrikes against ISIS destroyed much of Kobani. How do these events affect Ghalib's daily life?

2. When Hamza pressures Ghalib to go looting with him, how does Ghalib respond? What can you learn about their personalities from this exchange?

3. Why is Baba reluctant to leave Kobani despite his wife's plea? How do Baba's and Dayah's personalities and values influence the decisions they make?

4. Ghalib does not consider himself brave for saving Hamza's life. Do you think Ghalib is brave? What does bravery look like to you?

5. Ghalib and his family are Kurds, an ethnic minority. Give an example of how their background affects their decisions or their treatment during the journey.

6. Why does Ghalib feel so connected to Safaa when he first meets her? Why do you think Bushra is less receptive to Safaa?

7. What choice does Ghalib face after he ends up on the Turkish side of the border? If you were in Ghalib's position, what do you think you would have done and why?

8. How does Ghalib's relationship with Bushra change throughout the family's journey?

9. At the camp, Mohammad says that being afraid and being angry is sometimes the same thing. What do you think he means? What examples of this do you see in the book?

10. Why do Ghalib's parents decide to leave the refugee camp? Why is Bushra worried about going to Europe?

11. Before leaving Kobani, Ghalib insisted on bringing his video games and other "luxuries." What does Ghalib pack later when his family leaves the refugee camp? How and why has his approach changed?

12. Consider the story of Alan's birth and the story of Dapir's death. What do the two events have in common? What might have been different if the war in Syria had never happened?

13. What forms of discrimination do Ghalib's family face after they leave Kobani? How do their experiences relate to the title of the book?

14. Compare the representation of the characters in the book to portrayals of Middle Eastern refugees in the media. How is it similar or different?

15. Who are the characters in *Without Refuge* named after? Why do you think the author made this choice?

ABOUT THE AUTHOR

Jane Mitchell is an award-winning author of books for children and young people. *Without Refuge* was endorsed by Amnesty International Ireland for contributing to a better understanding of human rights.